Katie O'

If lost Please return
to Bronagh Murphy
P.7 Sliebh or 1 Rathgullion
Meigh Newry Co Down.

ARMAGH

Katie O'

Joyce A Stengel

POOLBEG
FOR CHILDREN

Published 2000
by Poolbeg Press Ltd
123 Baldoyle Industrial Estate
Dublin 13, Ireland
E-mail: poolbeg@iol.ie
www.poolbeg.com

© Joyce A Stengel 2000

Copyright for typesetting, layout, design
© Poolbeg Press Ltd

The moral right of the author has been asserted.

A catalogue record for this book is available from the British Library.

ISBN 1 85371 933 1

Cover design by Artmark
Illustration by Marianne Lee
Printed by The Guernsey Press Ltd,
Vale, Guernsey, Channel Islands.

About the Author

Joyce A Stengel lives with her husband in Connecticut, USA. They have two grown daughters and three grandchildren. She has written numerous articles which have appeared in various American magazines and newspapers, and is the author of *Kittiwake Bay, The Caribbean Jewels Mystery, Letting Go*, and *Sara Takes Charge*, all published by Poolbeg.

By the Same Author

Kittiwake Bay
Letting Go
The Caribbean Jewels Mystery
Sara Takes Charge

Published by Poolbeg

May 1852

1

Changes

Mam added potatoes to the soup kettle simmering over the turf fire. They made a small splash and the smell of soup filled our hut. Mam straightened up and wiped her hands on her apron. Her voice sounding worn and tired, she said, "'Tis decided, Katie love. You'll be going to America in Patrick's stead."

My heart thumped quick and hard. I held the bowl I'd been drying against my chest. America! School! Da! I'd see Da! But then . . . "Da sent the fare for Michael and Patrick," I said.

"Aye, that was the plan, Katie. Michael and Patrick this time. You and me to stay here with your Aunt Mary and Uncle Joseph till he's saved enough for us. But fate has a way of changing plans."

Mam gazed out the small window with her faraway look, the look she got when she thought of the potatoes rotting and changing everyone's plans, everyone's life.

My hands trembled. I set the bowl down carefully. I might be going to America! America – where there were schools and books. Fingers of guilt pricked me, "But, Mam, it's Patrick's turn and he's been wanting to go."

Mam nodded toward one of the curtains that divided the hut into four tiny sections – our living area, a sleeping space for Aunt Mary and Uncle Joseph, one for my two brothers, Michael, fifteen, and Patrick, sixteen, and one for Mam and me. The sound of Aunt Mary singing as she took her turn sitting with Patrick and sponging him came from behind one of the curtains.

"Katie, sure and you know," Mam said, lowering her voice, "Patrick's much too ill with fever to travel."

"But the ship's not leaving for two more weeks," I whispered back. "Sure Patrick will be better by then." But I wondered. Patrick, so tall and thin he looked like a walking-stick, and his nose always red and runny. And now, he'd been down on his cot for weeks. Just eating his soup wore him out.

My stomach fluttered. I wanted to go to America but not without Mam and not with Patrick sick. And I wanted to see Da but . . . "Will Da want me?" I asked.

Mam shook her head. "Of course he'll want you, Katie. He'll be mighty surprised to see how you've grown. You were just nine when he left. And here you are – all of fourteen years now." Still an uneasy feeling, a memory – me following Da around the farm, me trying to get his attention.

Clenching my hands in the folds of my skirt, I said, "It's Patrick's turn. Sure he'll be better in two weeks."

Mam breathed a long sigh. "God willing, but he'll not be strong enough for such a journey." She rubbed her eyes. "The smoke in this hovel never clears. My eyes are burning something fierce." She ran her hands through her greying brown hair, then guided me to the bench in front of the smouldering fire.

"Sit a minute, Katie," she said. She went to the fire to stir the steaming pot. Her shoulder blades rose like wings beneath the thin fabric of her dress. Would there ever be enough food in Ireland? I wondered. I jumped up and reached for the spoon. "Let me, Mam. You sit."

Handing me the spoon, she said, "I wish we had a lamb bone for the soup. Patrick needs nourishment."

I stirred the soup. It spattered and drops burned my hand. I rubbed my smarting fingers and went to sit on the bench with Mam. She put her arm about me and pulled me close. The peat fire burned quietly, heating the watery brew. The sound of Aunt Mary's humming filled the hut. Mam brushed my curls from my forehead and said as she'd said many a time before, "Your hair is just like my mother's was, an unruly mop of black curls." She smiled. "You do remind me of her. You've the same proud way about ye."

"I miss Granny," I murmured, thinking of my sharp-tongued Grandmother who had died last year. She had taught me and a few village children to read. My stomach tightened remembering how Da and Granny had often spat angry words. "Da didn't like Granny Shea, did he, Mam?"

Mam sighed. "They did lock horns. Your da thought Granny's love of learning a waste of time, and a way of putting on airs. And she just didn't understand him. Both of them stubborn and hot-tempered." She squeezed my shoulder. "And you've a temper yourself, Katie, love, as do all the O'Briens. You know how your granny wanted to be a teacher, just like you do. But she satisfied herself teaching you and the others that wanted to learn." She shook her head and sighed. "You're the only one in our family interested in book learning. Your brothers want nothing but to be out of doors working the land."

"Like Da," I said, remembering him frowning down at me when he caught me with a book and muttering such things as, "Uppity, useless nonsense".

3

Mam shifted on the bench and tilted my face towards her. "Father Shaughnessy's made all the necessary arrangements for you to go instead of Patrick. It's a golden opportunity, Katie. Father Shaughnessy says you're very bright, and you'll get more schooling there in America."

I sucked in my breath. "School," I breathed. "I'll really be going to school then?"

Mam smoothed my hair. "I should think so, love. Your da's a hard worker and he's doing well there in America. The little we hear from him through Mrs Reilly's letters are full of how grand it all is. You'll be living in a place much nicer than this hovel." She swept her hand around the smoky room, then smiled at me. "A opportunity."

So many feelings sped through me that my head spun. America! I couldn't wait to go, but then, Patrick – he should be going. And I didn't want to leave Mam. And then – Da. What would he say when he saw me instead of Patrick?

Oh, how I'd love to go to school! Granny used to read letters to me from a friend who had emigrated to America before the potatoes turned black, letters telling how her grandchildren were getting a fine education. Oh, it would be my dream come true to study all day long. My splash of joy flowed away as fast as it had come – Mam and Patrick wouldn't be there!

I swallowed hard. "When will you and Patrick come, Mam?"

"Just as soon as Patrick's well enough and your da sends the fare. It's more than three pounds five now. But with Michael working alongside him, it shouldn't take so long."

I jumped from the bench and went to the window. "I wonder will we ever be together again? Our whole family?" My voice squeaked and I cleared my throat.

Mam followed me to the door and stood beside me. Looking out, we could see Michael, his red hair blazing in the sun. He and Uncle Joseph, covered with muck, were leading the farm owner's old donkey, Dusty, from the bog, a load of turf on her back. "At least you and Michael will be together. The two of you have been like peas in a pod since the day you were born."

I grinned. "Aye, I'll be with Michael."

"Here, Katie, I want you to wear this." Mam reached up and took her Holy Family medal from around her neck. She slipped it over my head and the thin medal fell low on my chest. I fingered the engraved picture of the Holy Family, still warm from Mam's skin. "Mam, 'tis your own medal," I breathed.

She smiled and the little lines around her faded blue eyes crinkled. I reached out and touched them, wishing I could make the sadness go away.

Mam pulled me to her in a fierce hug. Her voice husky, she said, "Aye. And when you're missing me and Patrick, you remember how your mam promised we'd all be together again one day."

2

Aboard the Victor Darr

It was early morning in the dark hold. My body felt stiff from sleeping in such a cramped space. I heard Michael whistling "Molly Malone" as he left to queue up for one of the six cooking grates on deck. The deck – fresh air – I couldn't wait to get up there.

Little Maggie Shea wailed, adding to the noisy hubbub of the place. I dropped from our upper bunk to the damp wood planks. I took the little girl, not yet two, from Mrs Shea, following the morning routine we'd fallen into over the past two weeks. Michael cooked our ration and the Shea's ration of oatmeal; Mrs Shea queued for our rations of fresh water, and I cared for Maggie.

Her arms free, Mrs Shea brushed straggles of hair from her face. "Thank ye kindly, Katie." Her four bone-thin, tow-headed boys clustered about her. She picked up the water jugs and gave the boys a push toward the stairs. "Up with you now where we can breathe. Ach! The stink down here!"

"'Tis fierce," I said, snuggling Maggie against me. "And how's Brendan faring?"

Mrs Shea shook her head. "Some bit better," she said.

"Pray God, Maggie isn't with fever. She's been right fretful all the night long."

I pushed through the crowded, dark hold behind her and the boys – Brendan, six; Seamus, five; Aidan, four; and Niall, three. A rat scuttled by and Niall screamed. Seamus pulled him close and they scurried after their mother.

We'd journeyed with Mrs Shea and her children all the way from Cork. Her husband had died – "like as not starved to death," she'd told us, "giving his share of what little food there was to the children and me." She was going to Boston to be with her brother and his wife. Michael and I had helped her keep track of the five young'uns on the packet ship that plowed through rough water from Cork to Liverpool. We'd been right behind her for the medical exam just before we boarded the *Victor Darr*. Brendan had been flushed and whiney then, and Mrs Shea feared the doctors would turn them away. But the busy doctors had passed them on with barely a glance.

The ship had looked so big from the docks. We'd waited forever before they let us board, everyone pushing and shoving. The day grew hotter and hotter and tempers flared. Angry mutterings reached us and we passed them on to the people at the back. "Captain won't let us on till the cargo's stowed."

"Cargo's more important than us."

"They get their money from the cargo."

"They make plenty on us."

"For sure, I'm told they don't feed ye half what ye paid for."

Finally the order had come to board. Michael scooped up Niall, I held Maggie tight against me, and Mrs Shea clutched the other three boys to her. Somehow, dragging our bundles and

and the children, we made it to the main deck. Some people scrambled up the sides of the ship and fell in. "Man overboard," someone screamed. A sailor yelled, "Let 'em swim." I wondered – had the people made it? Had they drowned?

Finally, hundreds of us had crammed the main deck A porter opened the hatch and others, smelling of grog and swearing oaths, herded us down the hatch. Michael elbowed his way through the crush and saved a berth for us. I hated it down in the hold, "tween decks" the sailors called it, rats all about, water seeping through the planks, no portholes, the only air and light what came in from the hatches.

A woman retched nearby, bringing my thoughts back to the present. Carrying Maggie, I pushed on through the hold, past the rows of platform berths stacked on top of each other and close together. Someone moaned. So many thin, pale faces looked out from the berths. So many of them too sick to go on deck. I thanked the Lord that the sickness that had made my head ache and set my stomach in a jumble had passed after the first few days.

A group of unshaven men sat on chests smoking tea-leaves. The smoke thickened the air and made it even harder to breathe, but the men claimed it helped keep down disease. Everyone feared an outbreak of dysentery, or worse, cholera. No air, no place to relieve yourself, just the two huts on the outside deck where you had to wait for ages. Down here people had to use a pot. And no water to wash, unless we used our precious drinking water. How could we keep clean?

The ship rolled steeply. Clutching Maggie tight, I slid into a stout woman. She murmured something soothing in what sounded like German and steadied me. I gained my footing and hurried up the plank stairs.

The chill wind that sprang from the ocean felt wonderful. I tucked the edge of my red shawl around Maggie. She lay in my arms, staring up at me with big eyes. I made faces and cooed to her. Her tiny mouth curved in a smile. Her little body radiated heat. She did feel feverish.

I stood at the rail, where others stared down into the water or talked in little groups. Wind filled the dingy, grey sails, and the big, heavy ship ploughed through waves that crashed against its sides making it creak and groan. The wind was sharp and I felt Maggie tremble. I left the rail and picked my way through the people – some huddled about pots of oatmeal, some stretched out sleeping – to the snug spot I liked behind a small shed. I wrapped Maggie in my shawl and cradled her head on my lap. She soon fell into a fitful sleep. I pulled *Robinson Crusoe* from my pocket. It would be awhile before Michael and Mrs Shea came back with the oatmeal and water. Soon I was with Robinson Crusoe on his lonely island.

"So there ye are, Katie O'Brien, back with Rob's adventures, are you?"

I looked up and smiled. There towered tall, lanky Mr O'Donnell, with his wiry, dark brown beard. His forehead was so high, the hair seemed to spring from the crown of his head. His bright blue eyes were sharp and twinkling. He loved reading as much as I did and thought it wonderful that I'd be going to school in America. He looked to sea, lifted his head and tapped his fingers against each other, a pose he struck when he was going to quote something from a book.

In rolling words, he said, "'*Some books are to be tasted, others to be swallowed, and some few to be chewed and digested.*'"

"Did that Will Shakespeare you told me about say that?"

"Not this one. Those words were uttered by one Francis Bacon."

The ship gave a sudden lurch, jarring Maggie awake. She wailed. I scooped her up and she wound her thin little arms round my neck and snuggled into my shoulder. I crooned to her and rubbed her bony back.

Mr O'Donnell pulled a biscuit from the sack of extra food he'd brought with him. "Give this to the wee lass."

I pried Maggie's hands from my hair and gave her the biscuit. She turned her head and whimpered.

"I wouldn't be surprised but we're heading for a storm. Look at that sky," Mr O'Donnell said, folding his long body down next to me.

The sky did look dark in the distance, but the ship settled down into its usual roll. Maggie burrowed against me and sucked her thumb.

"Just think, Mr O'Donnell, what it would be like to be stranded on an island all alone. At least when we get to America we'll be with other people."

"Aye, people can be a great comfort. Or a great curse. I've travelled far and wide and have found men are the same – some good, some bad. 'Tis best to stick with the good and avoid the bad."

"Did Will Shakespeare say that?"

Mr O'Donnell laughed. "Not that I know of. Yours truly says that from years of living. But I venture to guess Will would agree with me. 'Tis good advice, lass."

"Are you thinking of Ireland, then?"

He leaned his head back against the wood, his whiskered chin pointing upwards, his eyes closed, his long, restless fingers drumming the deck. He sat that way so long I thought he wasn't going to answer me. Finally, he spoke. "Aye. I've left my loved ones behind." He told me of his parents, his father a Scot and his mother Irish. They had died when their cottage was torched by the overseer who worked for an English owner. He'd travelled to Scotland after that, where he taught school, then back to Ireland, where he met and married the love of his life. He'd worked in a lawyer's office in Galway and rented a room above the office.

Then, in 1845, the potatoes failed. "The lawyer stayed on till '47, then left for America. The hunger, lass, the hunger that swept through Ireland, gnawed at our bellies. My wife and I had longed for a child, but through the years the Lord had not given us that joy. Then my wife found she was with child. But weak as she was, she soon lost the babe and her own life." He heaved a great sigh. "After that, I stowed away on a ship to England. I found a post in a boys' school and set about saving for this voyage."

We sat silent for a few minutes. Then I told him my story – the part I remembered, and the part I'd heard from Mam.

We'd been tenant farmers before the potatoes went bad. We'd rented our own piece of land to farm and had a cow and a few pigs. We'd lived in a cottage that Mam made cozy and warm. Then the potatoes rotted right in the field. They hung brown and soggy on thin white roots. And the stink of them! Mam said the rot spread right across Ireland like a plague, leaving people starving and dying right in the streets.

Our own Bridget had died. She was two years younger than me. She used to follow me about like another shadow. She'd burned with fever then got weaker and weaker. I remembered Mam washing her body for burial. Mam never made a sound but tears streamed down her face. Da hadn't cried. He shouted and cursed, then grew silent as he dug a grave.

In no time at all Da couldn't pay the rent. Our landlord, who lived in England, evicted us, "shovelled us out," Mam said. Da had worked building new roads in the countryside. Our

11

meals got worse and worse – a bit of cabbage or turnip in a pot of water. Da's money did no good. There was no food to buy. Then there was no work for Da at all. Between the little we had and borrowing the rest from Father Shaughnessy, Da scraped together the three pounds five for the voyage to America. We'd heard the streets there were lined with gold. Once there, Da would find work. He'd pay Father Shaughnessy back, then send for us.

We became cottiers along with Uncle Joseph and Aunt Mary. We worked for a tenant farmer. Our pay was the right to live in that smoky hut and the use of a garden patch to farm. How we hated it, especially Michael. "We're nothing more than beggars working to fill our bellies," he'd say bitterly. "'Tis no way to live. There's no pride in it."

"Katie." Michael's excited voice stopped me. He strode toward us, carrying a bowl of oatmeal. "Katie, I've just been talking to a fellow who's going out west when we get to America. Morning, Mr O'Donnell," he said, nodding to the older man. "The man I met – he says that the land goes on and on as far as the eye can see." He tilted his chin toward the water. "Just like this endless Atlantic Ocean."

"Maggie's ailing, Michael. Sing to her," I pleaded. "She loves it when you sing. Sing her my song – 'Katie O'.""

"Katie, did ye hear me about the land?" Michael asked, reaching into his pocket for his feeding bowl and spoon. He spooned some oatmeal into his bowl and fed Maggie a small bit. She tongued it out.

I busied myself, pulling my bowl and spoon from my pocket and taking some of the thick gruel. It was tasteless and settled like a cold lump in my stomach. All the time, I was thinking, *No, Michael, no! You can't go traveling out west and leave me alone with Da.*

"Katie O'," Michael said.

I looked up at him. He tugged my hair. "Don't be fretting that I'll be taking off for the west soon as we arrive in America. I'll be working on the docks with Da, helping save for Mam and Patrick's passage, but some day . . ."

Mr O'Donnell stood up and stretched. "Some day, Michael, you will own your own bit of land, and you, Katie, will be the schoolteacher you hope to become. You are both questing, like Odysseus. You, Michael, quest land, and you, Katie, quest knowledge."

I wrinkled my forehead. "Who's Odysseus?"

Mr O'Donnell winked at me. "A story for another time."

Mrs Shea's voice reached us before she did. "Dig out your cups, boys," she said, "Michael's there with breakfast."

The ship gave another sudden lurch and Mrs Shea, lugging the two water jugs, sort of slid toward us. Mr O'Donnell steadied her and took one of the heavy jugs. "Ah, we must preserve the nectar of life."

Mrs Shea frowned. She'd told me he seemed nice enough but he did talk crazy-like. "It's a bit quieter here in this spot away from the wind," she said, pulling out her own cup. "But one of the sailors is shouting to go below decks. We're heading into a storm, he says."

I looked out at the sea. We'd set sail two weeks before and it would be another two or three weeks before we'd see land again. We'd run into a few squalls but no big storms. Now threatening clouds rolled toward us.

Mr O'Donnell took Niall on his lap, who wailed in protest till Mr O'Donnell spooned oatmeal into his mouth. "When these storms come they blow in fast. Eat quickly, then we'd best go below."

Sharp waves rose high. The ship plunged up then down,

sliding me against Mrs Shea. We quickly ate our gruel and washed it down with a half cup of water. It looked like ditch water and tasted terrible. I choked a little more down.

Mr O'Donnell grimaced as he drank. "This nectar tastes very much like vinegar. I would guess it is stored in wine casks and vinegar has been added to stop spoilage."

"And then they only fill the jugs halfway," Mrs Shea complained.

Wind-swollen rain swept across the deck. I wrapped my shawl tight about Maggie and ducked her head against my shoulder.

"This storm's gonna be a big one," a man shouted.

A woman stared at the black clouds, crossed herself and began to moan.

The ship bucked again. We rushed into action. Michael picked up the oatmeal bowls and our water jug. Mr O'Donnell scooped Niall into his arms. Mrs Shea took her jug and shouted to the boys to hold fast together. I carried Maggie. We left our sheltered spot and a gust of wind blasted us.

Sailors ran about, shouting, "All passengers below."

"Water! We need fresh water!" someone cried.

Sailors herded us toward the steerage hatch. "Down with you. Down. All passengers must go below."

We clambered down the stairs into the hold. Lanterns, that hung from the ceiling, swung wildly, throwing freakish shadows. The stink of all those unwashed bodies and vomit hit me like a solid wall. I thought about the passengers in the few first-class cabins. Imagine! A whole cabin for one or two people. I didn't mind steerage when we could be out on deck, but down here . . .

The ship bucked sharply sending trunks, pots, pans, jugs

14

and cans scuttling across the floor. People cried out and scurried to find their possessions.

I clutched Maggie to me and followed Michael past the rows of berths to ours.

"Over here, boys! Over here," Mrs Shea cried.

Brendan stood by the berth, waiting for Michael to boost him up.

Niall whined, "Katie, Katie!"

It was four to a berth so we shared ours with the children. Mr O'Donnell placed Niall on the top berth then disappeared into the dark hold to find his own cramped space.

I handed Maggie, still crying fitfully, to her mother. "I think she is ailing, Mrs Shea. She's warm to the touch."

"Mother of God," Mrs Shea mumbled.

Michael boosted me and Brendan onto the upper platform. He hoisted himself up and lay on his side as there wasn't enough head room for him to sit.

The ship heaved. I grabbed Niall to keep him from rolling off the edge. The sounds of people shouting, crying and praying bounced off the walls. Angry voices rolled through the hold. "They've locked us in!"

"They'll not open the hatch till the storm's over."

"Water! We need fresh water!"

"You'll not get it till the storm's done."

"We're locked in!"

I lay on my side, Niall curved in the shelter of my arm, listening to the ship creak and groan. A monstrous wave slammed the ship's side, shifting and tilting it, plunging us from one side of the berth to the other. Nearby, someone retched. Vomit splattered the floor, adding to the already sour smell. Sobbing, Niall clung to me. I tried to comfort him, tried to keep my own fear bottled inside.

Thunder exploded and the ship shuddered till I thought its boards would split. My breath stopped with terror. I hugged Niall to me. The noise of the storm and people crying out clattered against my ears. A high-pitched wail sounded close by.

The platform dipped, then straightened. Michael moved Brendan next to Niall, then squeezed beside him. He reached across the squirming boys and clasped my arm with his big, warm hand. "Katie! Katie O'! We'll be all right," he said firmly.

The wailing stopped and I realized it had been me.

Wedged tightly together, Michael's hand on my arm, I half dreamt, half remembered images of home. The afternoon when I'd known for sure that I'd be going to America in Patrick's stead played before my eyes.

I ran from the hut through the green fields, over the old stone bridge, past the flowering bushes to the lough. I sat on my favourite rock, thoughts and feelings surging like water in a rushing stream. I wanted to go to America, but then, I didn't want to leave Mam. I gazed out at a lone fisherman working his oars and gliding his boat over the clear water. After a time, the steady slap of water and the rhythmic movement of his oars calmed me. A quiet excitement burned in my centre. I was going to America! I was going to school!

The ship rose, then plunged. The woman in the next berth screamed, *"Holy Mother! We're going down! We'll drown for sure."*

Niall shifted and his weight pressed the Holy Family medal against my skin. Please, God, I prayed silently. Let us make it to America.

3

Burial at Sea

The sun sank into the western sea leaving purple streaks in the darkening sky. A stiff wind snapped the sails and gooseflesh rippled my skin. I moved closer to Michael. He took my hand and squeezed hard. Mrs Shea, two boys on either side of her, looked numb. A few of the ragged, skeletal passengers gathered round, weeping and wailing like at a wake back home.

The storm had raged for two endless days. All that time we'd been locked below in steerage with only the water and food we had with us. The nasty smells of the place had clogged the air and spread sickness. This morning the sea had calmed and the sailors had unlocked the hatch. Little Maggie lay dead in her mother's arms. Hours later, a bearded, beefy sailor had wrapped her body in canvas, then placed it in a sack weighted with stones. Now he carried her shrouded body to the rail and rested his arms against it. In a gruff voice he asked, "Does anyone want to say a prayer?"

Mrs Shea, her thin face drawn and pale, stared at him and, her voice hoarse and whispery, said, "Sure there must be a priest on board?"

The boys clung to her and looked at the small sack laying limp across the sailor's arms with huge, frightened eyes.

"No priest." The sailor lifted his arms and held Maggie's body over the choppy water.

Mr O'Donnell stepped forward. "Wait," he commanded. His long fingers made the sign of the cross over the sad bundle. "In the name of the Father, the Son and the Holy Ghost, may this child rest in peace."

"*Amen,*" the group echoed. Many hands fluttered like white birds as the people crossed themselves.

The sailor dropped Maggie's slight body. I watched it tumble down, down, down. It hit the black water with barely a splash and disappeared. I gazed at the ocean trying to mark the spot and saw Da lowering Bridget's body into the ground.

4

Arrival

Seagulls whirled and cried overhead. I clutched the ship's rail and leaned into the wind blowing off the water. The rail was wet and slippery. I squeezed it hard, trying to still the jitters buzzing through me like bees in a bottle. The lumpy coastline grew into a long clutter of buildings. My breath caught in my throat. Soon I'd be in America!

Someone shouted, "Boston! There's Boston!" Other voices took up the cry. Fellow passengers squashed me against the rail.

Michael, standing beside me, slipped his arm about my shoulders. Raising his voice above the clamour of the crowd, he cried, "America, Katie O'. We made it!"

"We made it," I echoed softly.

Dysentery had swept through the ship, weakening people and leading to several deaths besides little Maggie's. We were stick-thin and our worn clothes smelled terrible. Some of the passengers hadn't passed the doctor's inspection. What would happen to them? Would they be sent back to England?

I stared straight ahead, filling my eyes with my first view of America. I could make out signs that read *Grain, Meal & Feed, Fish, Flour, O'Toole's Saloon*, on buildings lining the waterfront. Horse-drawn carts and wagons rumbled up and down the wharf, their beds piled high with boxes. As we drew closer, the air grew heavy and hot. A wet, fishy smell filled the air. My clothes stuck to me and sweat trickled through my hair.

Sailors shouted instructions for disembarking and herded us from the boat. People, eager to leave the foul-smelling ship, pushed and shoved, crushing me.

A bony man thrust his sharp elbows between Michael and me, separating us. I tried to squeeze past him but a woman with children clinging to her skirt nearly trampled me. The smell of their unwashed bodies filled my nose and stopped my breath.

The crowd caught me up and moved me slowly down the gangplank. The sticky air clung to my skin. Heart racing, I clutched my bundle, straining for a glimpse of Michael.

Once on the wharf, I dodged crates and barrels and men pushing handcarts. Some men and boys carried big signs. A ragged boy grasped my arm. His fingers dug into my flesh. "Looking for a place are ya, miss? I knows a cheap boardin' house."

I pulled away from him and ran down the docks. Finally, the press of people thinned and I spotted Michael searching for me. I ran to him, dropped my bundle and threw my arms about him.

He hugged me so tight my breath puffed out. Then he tilted my chin and smiled into my eyes. "Don't fret, Katie O'. I'd have found ye. But stay close. I don't want to lose ye 'mongst this swarm of people." Stepping back and stretching his neck, he scanned the bustling wharf. "Now to find Da."

I edged closer to him. I'd not lose sight of him again, I vowed. All around me people called and shouted to each other in a mix of foreign tongues. Was America big enough for all these people?

I spotted Mrs Shea and her boys with a man and woman. The woman knelt by the children and hugged each one to her. The man embraced Mrs Shea .

I nudged Michael. "There's Mrs Shea with her brother and his wife."

Michael shook his head. "'Twas a hard trip for her, losing little Maggie."

I nodded. I remembered the clasp of Maggie's thin arms about my neck. Then the image of her body hurtling down into the black water flashed before me. I shut my eyes tight, squeezing it away.

Trying to forget, I opened my eyes and looked about the busy wharf. The smell of fish filled was powerful. Snorting horses pulled wagons driven by shouting men. Men called to each other as they unloaded cargo. The sounds clattered against my ears. I scanned the crowd of people. How would we ever find Da in this busy place? Would I recognize him?

Two men, carrying signs, were shouting at a newly arrived family. The woman started crying and pulled her sons close to her. Her husband grabbed their bundles and they hurried down the dock. The men, one fleshy and dark with a patch over his left eye, the other, younger and strong-looking, came closer. The younger one, with his pointy face and buck teeth, looked like a weasel. As I read their signs, my heart caught in my throat.

"*Irish, Go Home! America for Americans!*"

"*Jobs for Native Born Americans! Immigrants Not Wanted!*"

My stomach tightened. I tugged on Michael's sleeve. "Michael, those signs! They don't want us here in America!"

Michael glanced at the men. The fat one saw us looking

and shouted, "Go on back on the boat. There's no jobs here for foreign paupers. Go back where you belong!"

Michael tensed and his brows drew together.

"Don't answer, Michael," I pleaded, pulling him away from the angry-looking men. They had nothing to do with us, I told myself. "Oh, why isn't Da here, Michael?" I couldn't wait to see him. But then, I thought, he's expecting Patrick, not me.

With a shaky hand, I pressed the Holy Family medal against my chest.

Michael glared at the men, who were yelling at other immigrants.

I yanked on his arm. "Michael, what will Da say when he sees me?"

Sweat darkened his red hair and plastered it against his forehead. He looked at me, his blue eyes steady. "Da will be glad ye've come, Katie O'. Why do ye worry so?" He jerked his head over his shoulder. "And pay no mind to those scoundrels with the signs."

Little shivers rippled through me. I wished we were home. Nobody wanted us here! Da was nowhere in sight! I thought of the letter packed in my bundle, the letter Mam had written explaining why I'd come instead of Patrick. Sure Michael was right. Da would be happy to see me.

A man crying, "Meat-pies! Hot meat-pies!" pushed his handbarrow along the wharf. My mouth watered and my stomach grumbled.

Michael thrust his hands in his pockets, pulled them out empty. "No meat-pies for us."

I shrugged but how I longed to bite into a meat-pie. "Michael, doesn't that handbarrow bring to mind you pushing me in the wheelbarrow back home and singing to me?"

Michael's ginger-coloured brows danced and, softly, he sang, "Molly Malone", changing the name as always to Katie O'.

"In Dublin's fair city, where the girls are so pretty,
'Twas there that I first met sweet Katie O'.
She drove a wheelbarrow thro' streets broad and narrow,
Crying 'Cockles and mussels, alive, alive o'.
Alive, alive o! Alive, alive o!
Crying 'Cockles and mussels, alive, alive o!'"

"I heard a fine tenor, Michael O'Brien, and knew it was you. And with you would be Miss Katie O'Brien." Mr O'Donnell held out a meat-pie to each of us. "I bring you delicacies from the pie-peddler making his way across these boards."

"Oh, Mr O'Donnell, how kind of you," I said, biting into the hot pasty. The crust flaked and the hot filling burst into my mouth, burning my tongue. My stomach lurched and bile poured into my mouth. I felt as sick as I had the first day at sea.

"You're looking a bit green, Katie," Mr O'Donnell said. "Take small bites. Eat slowly."

Michael downed his pie in a bite or two with no sign of feeling sick. He held out his hand to Mr O'Donnell. "Thank you, sir. 'Twas most generous of you."

Mr O'Donnell nodded and wiped a few crumbs from his wiry beard. "A cool glass of grog would follow nicely." He wiped his neck with a soiled handkerchief. "And where is your father, may I ask? Was he not meeting you?"

"He should be here," Michael answered, scanning the docks with worried eyes.

The blare of a ship's whistle shuddered through me, right down to my toes. I glanced out at the sea. Dark clouds moved in and covered the sun, but the moist air stayed hot and suffocating. A gull swooped and snatched bread from a small boy's hand. The boy wailed. Other gulls circled and cackled.

A hurrying man bumped into me then rushed on. I looked up at Mr O'Donnell, tapping his fingers together as he studied Michael and me.

"You need not worry about us, sir. If our da's not here soon, Katie has his address and we'll ask the way," Michael said, gathering up his bundle. He laid his hand on my shoulder. "Come on, Katie, we'll walk a bit." Tall and straight, he started up the dock.

I took up my bundle. "Goodbye, Mr O'Donnell. Thank you again for the meat-pie."

Mr O'Donnell picked up his black bag and fell into step with me. "As it so happens I am going in the same direction. I am in search of a pub for a pint of grog."

We walked down the wharf, Michael whistling "Molly Malone". The wharf seemed to sway beneath us, like the deck of the ship. I tripped over a coil of rope and bumped into a post. Mr O'Donnell laughed and said I still had "sea legs". People all around us were hugging friends or relatives. They laughed and shouted greetings. Little by little, they left the docks. Ships sailed into and out of the harbour. The air smelled of salt and sea. A soft warm drizzle began to fall.

Footsteps pounded behind us. Rough hands pushed me into Michael, sending us both sprawling. Patch-eye snatched Mr O'Donnell's bag and fled. Weasel-face, who had pushed me, ran after him.

Mr O'Donnell and Michael, shouting, *"Stop! Thief!"* sprang after them.

The fleeing men tore in front of a horse cart. The horse reared, pawed the air and snorted. The driver flicked the reins and the cart swayed and rumbled over the wooden planks.

I scooped up my bag and dragging Michael's hurried after them. Just outside a tumbledown shack with a crooked sign reading, *Rooster's Grog Shop*, Michael was jumping onto Patch-eye's back.

Weasel-face lifted his sign and aimed at Michael.

Mr O'Donnell charged into him. The sign hit the ground with a clatter.

Men rushed from the saloon to aid Michael and Mr O'Donnell.

I stood frozen, my heart thundering in my chest, watching fists fly and men fall and roll on the ground. I saw Michael draw his big hand back into a fist. Shouting, "Ye'll not push my sister about and get away with it," he smashed his fist square on Weasel-face's mouth. Blood spurted.

Outnumbered, Patch-eye and Weasel-face grabbed their signs and scooted down the waterfront. Before they disappeared into an alley, Weasel-face turned and, blood making his voice thick, screamed, "You'll be sorry ya came here, ya Micks."

I spotted Mr O'Donnell's black bag and dashed for it. Panting, I lugged the heavy satchel back to him.

A burly, red-faced man with a soiled white apron covering his huge middle came out of the saloon. He pulled Mr O'Donnell to his feet. "I'm Rooster and it's a real pleasure to meet you gentlemen." He shook Michael's hand.

Michael's right eye looked puffy.

Two pretty ladies all dressed up in the fanciest clothes I'd ever seen had been watching the fight. The one with yellow curls winked at Michael. Michael reddened. The women laughed and, skirts swaying, walked slowly back into the saloon.

"You're both welcome to come in for a pint – on the house," Rooster said.

Mr O'Donnell glanced down at me. "Ah, here's young Katie with my worldly goods," he cried. He opened the bag and, chuckling, pulled out books. "I think our would-be thieves would have been sorely disappointed when they found my treasures. I'd venture to guess they don't know the value of books."

I reached for one of the books and smoothed my hand over its cover.

"Mr O'Donnell, you told me someone said 'The pen is mightier than the sword'. But look at you!"

Mr O'Donnell glanced from the books to me. "I still think that, Katie. But people have to listen to the words for them to do any good."

Rooster threw back his big head and laughed. I could see black spaces where some of his teeth were missing. "I agree with you one hundred percent, sir. I could use a man like you, and you, too," he said to Michael. "You must just be off the boat?"

"That we are," said Mr O'Donnell, dabbing at his bloody mouth with his handkerchief. "And quite an unusual welcome we have received."

Rooster scratched his nearly bald head. "Not unusual. The Know-Nothings were out in force today. They're always there to 'greet' a new shipload of immigrants. It's them and their foul ideas we're fighting."

"Look, Michael," I shouted.

All three men followed my pointing finger.

A pencil-thin woman flew down the waterfront through the warm rain. She was holding up a sign that read, *Patrick and Michael O'Brien*.

26

5

To the Tenement

I ran after the woman, who was hurrying past the saloon. "Wait! Michael O'Brien is right here. And I'm Katie. I came in Patrick's stead. Wait! Please!"

The woman stopped, then darted towards me. A drop of water hung from the tip of her long sharp nose. Her grey hair was pulled into a hard knot at the back of her head. "Where's Michael O'Brien?" she demanded.

Michael caught up to us. "I'm Michael O'Brien. Who are you? Where . . . where's our da?"

The woman's mouth tightened and she shook her head. "Hurt. Happened at work."

Michael gasped. "Is he hurt bad?"

The woman sniffed and shook her head. "'Tis his foot. I'm Mrs Reilly. I . . ."

"Oh, you're the lady that writes the letters for Da," I interrupted.

Mrs Reilly glanced at me and nodded. "That's right. We live in the same tenement." Her eyes scooted back to Michael. "Yer certainly an O'Brien. Red hair, blue eyes, same as your da. Spittin' image." Her brow creased as she studied me. "But where's the other one? Yer da said two sons, Michael, fifteen, and Patrick, sixteen."

I looked up at her. "Patrick couldn't come. I came in his stead."

Mrs Reilly looked puzzled.

"Our Patrick got the fever," Michael explained, squinting through his one good eye. "So our sister, Katie here, came in his place."

Mrs Reilly's eyes went round. "Sister? Yer da never mentioned a daughter."

My heart fell to my feet. Had Da forgotten all about me?

Mrs Reilly peered at Michael. "Yer eye's swollen. Been fightin', have ye?"

Michael shuffled his feet. "Some men . . . carrying signs . . . they . . ."

"Ach! The Know-Nothings. So they were here, were they? Sticking their noses everywhere these days."

"What are Know-Nothings?" I asked.

"Thugs! That's what they are. It's them hurt yer da."

"Why?" I asked.

"They say the Irish are taking their jobs, taking over the country. Ye'll hear plenty about 'em."

"Know-Nothings. 'Tis odd sounding."

"They're really members of the American Party. But they're real secret like. When anyone asks 'em something, they say they know nothing. Fools! That's what they are . . . and we are too, standing here in the rain." She pulled out a sack she'd been holding under her apron. "I've a bit of bread and cheese. Best we get out of the wet." She dashed off toward a shed with an overhang, calling over her shoulder, "Have a bite to eat, then I'll take ye to yer da."

The rain fell quietly, sending up steamy odours from the

wood planks. Michael and I crouched in the shed doorway and Mrs Reilly handed each of us a wedge of hard cheese and a chunk of damp bread. I took a small bite of the cheese and rolled its tastiness around in my mouth.

Mrs Reilly, standing, hands on hips, said to Michael, "Ye'll be a help – big and strong. That is if ye can find work." She turned to me and frowned. "A girl, then. And how old are ye?"

I pulled my shoulders back. "Fourteen."

"Sure and that's old enough to work, God willing ye find a place."

"But I'll be going to school. Mam said so."

Mrs Reilly snorted. "Did she now? Ye'll have to talk to yer da about that."

Her words and tone started a worry in my mind. Would Da not want me to go to school?

Michael stood and heaved his bundle over his shoulder. I picked mine up and hugged it to me. We followed Mrs Reilly down the creaky steps into the soft rain. In front of the saloon, I stopped and looked over to where Mr O'Donnell and Rooster stood talking.

Mr O'Donnell picked up his bag and walked over to us. "Ah, I've been waiting to bid you *adieu*. So then, my friends, have you gotten everything sorted out?"

I glanced at Mrs Reilly. "Mrs Reilly here tells us our Da's hurt his foot and couldn't come for us. She's going to take us to him."

Mr O'Donnell nodded to Mrs Reilly. He shook Patrick's hand then smiled down at me. "I dare say, Miss Katie O'Brien, we shall see each other again as we pursue our adventures in this fine city of Boston."

I smiled. "Just like Robinson Crusoe."

He nodded. "Like Robinson Crusoe." He picked up his

bag and started towards *Rooster's Grog Shop*, then turned to say, "Remember what I said, Katie, about people being the same the world over?"

I nodded.

"It is unfortunate that on our arrival to our new country, we met with two of the bad. But take heart! We are sure to encounter the good." He gave me a little salute and walked away.

I wish he were my da, I thought, then flushed feeling that I'd betrayed my own da.

Mrs Reilly, who'd been staring, wide-eyed and open-mouthed, at Mr O'Donnell, snapped her mouth shut. "Sure and he's a fine looking gentleman, even with his mouth all swollen. And doesn't he talk fine!"

She gave her head a little shake, then set off at a brisk pace. Michael kept up with her but I had to take fast, running hops. We continued down the waterfront, Michael humming or singing low under his breath. I caught the strains of "The Minstrel Boy" and "Believe Me, If All Those Endearing Young Charms". The tunes filled me with sadness, making me yearn for home.

But then there was so much to look at! We passed offices, counting houses, work-shops, markets and saloon after saloon. Singing came from some of the saloons, angry shouting from others. Wagons and carts clattered by. The noise of the place rose and fell.

Many piers jutted into the sea. At one pier, a group of people clustered round a fishing boat, calling out to the fishermen. Mrs Reilly whipped her hand toward the crowd. "Must have had a good catch today. This is where ye get yer fish, when ye've the money for it. If ye get it from the pushcarts, ye can't be sure it's fresh."

Farther down the docks grew quieter. Michael stopped humming and pointed to a sign. "That say Lincoln's Wharf, Katie?"

I followed his pointing finger. "Aye." Michael could read a bit.

He nodded. "I thought so. That's where Da works."

I looked down the wide wharf and thought of Da working there every day. And far away on the other side of the ocean were Mam and Patrick. The thought of all that water separating us made me miss them so much my stomach hurt. I pressed my fingers against my medal, remembering Mam's voice saying how we'd all be together one day. How I wished Mam was here beside me now, in this strange, new country.

We crossed the road separating the docks from a jumble of buildings and tramped up a narrow street, the cobblestones dark and wet. A woman dragging a screaming boy passed us and they disappeared into one of the buildings. Other tattered children raced about, unmindful of the falling night and the rain. A few, skinny as scarecrows, stood and stared at us. Dark alleys stretched between buildings. I plodded along, my legs feeling heavier and heavier. Michael tweaked one of my plaits. "Sure and it can't be much further, Katie O'."

"I'm all right, Michael," I said, willing my tired feet forward.

At a square Mrs Reilly waited for us. Nearby, a group of men crowded around a man waving his arms and shouting.

My heart pulsed in my throat. "Mrs Reilly, are they Know-Nothings?"

"Not up here. That one waving his arms like a madman – that's Dennis O'Malley, a *friend* of yer da's." From the way she said *friend*, I could tell she didn't like the man.

She bounded up another steep street. We hurried after her, through alleyways where kids called to each other from

31

tiny iron porches that looked like to fall in a brisk wind. In one of the alleys, I saw a ragged man searching through rubbish. A rat scuttled from behind a barrel. And the smell! 'Twas enough to make me gag.

I thought of the green fields and the blue lough back home. We'd come to America for a better life, but this . . . "Mrs Reilly, sure Da can't live round here.!"

Mrs Reilly stopped and, looking somewhat shamefaced, said, "Aye. 'Tis where we live."

"But the letters . . ."

"Don't I know about the letters, for isn't it myself that wrote the words to yer mam. But, yer da, he's got his pride ye know. He insisted I make things sound good like, thinking they'd be that way before any of ye came over." She made a satisfied sound. "I'll finally be moving from this rat-infested place myself. Before the first snowfall of the season, I'll be over in Charlestown."

I pondered on what she'd said. Da had lied? Not really lied, just exaggerated. He'd wanted to make things sound better for Mam's sake. But what about school? My legs felt like iron weights and my bundle, too. The warm spring rain trickled down my neck and soaked through my clothes. Sure Da would want me to go to school like Mam did. Suddenly, I had a feeling that Mam was there beside me. I smiled, feeling warm inside.

I stumbled. Michael stopped his whistling and caught me. "Watch your step, Katie. 'Tis tired ye are, I know. Soon ye'll be able to rest."

At last, Mrs Reilly stopped in front of a tall wooden building. "Here we are," she said.

I drew in my breath and grasped Michael's hand. What would Da say when he saw me instead of Patrick?

6

Reunion with Da

Mrs Reilly pushed open the door. A heavy smell of people and food, almost as bad as on the ship, struck me. Michael and I crowded into a stale hallway, darker than the deepening dusk outside. A droning noise, like bees in a hive, filled the air. How many people lived here? A steep flight of wooden stairs leaned against the left wall. Upstairs, a door slammed. A woman shouted. A baby cried. To the right of the stairs, a passage disappeared into blackness. The street door closed behind us. I felt Michael's hand tremble.

Mrs Reilly rapped on a door to the right and pushed it open. I caught the sweet smell of pipe tobacco. An image of Da filling and tapping down his pipe sprang to mind.

"Patrick! Michael!" Da called. "Come here, let me see you. Aggie, light the lamp. I want to see my sons."

Mrs Reilly bustled in and lit an oil lamp in the centre of the table. The light threw giant shadows on the walls. The hot, airless room smelled sour under the sweet tobacco smell. The lamp-light played on wide cracks crawling down colourless walls. A small iron stove and a coal bucket stood against the back wall. A sink with a shelf of crockery over it, stood next to the stove. A boarded window on the front wall blocked light and air. Beneath the window was a bed with a sagging mattress. The table and four mismatched chairs occupied the centre of the room. Da's large frame loomed in one of the chairs. His bandaged right foot rested on an upside-down bucket. His face was lost in shadow. I hid behind Michael.

"Michael! Sure it must be you! Come here," Da said gruffly. He clasped Michael's hand and drew him down to him, studied his face. "How you've grown! And where's Patrick?" Brows knit, he peered round Michael at me.

Michael straightened up and drew me forward. I tried to smile but my lips wobbled. "Our Patrick got the fever, Da," Michael explained. "He couldn't come, so Father Shaughnessy helped Mam get Katie on the boat in his place."

"Katie?" he said, staring at me.

I started toward him.

He turned to Michael. "But Patrick! Is he bad off? And how is yer mother?" He squinted in the dim light. "What happened to yer eye?"

I froze to the spot and twisted my hands.

Mrs Reilly interrupted. "I'll go up to my place and get the stew I left simmering," she said. "Real Irish stew 'tis, made with mutton."

Da smiled and nodded at Mrs Reilly. "Aggie Reilly, 'tis a kind soul ye are. It'll be my loss when ye move on."

"Ach! You'll get yer own place one day soon, Seán O'Brien."

Da frowned and shook his head. "Maybe. If things don't keep setting me back." He glared at me and I knew I was one of the things setting him back. I knew he didn't want me here.

"Yer looking more and more like yer granny Shea," he said to me. He turned to Michael. "Tell me, Michael, how is Patrick?"

Michael nodded toward me. "Katie there has a letter from Mam."

I stumbled over my words. "M . . . Mam's real worried about Patrick. He's down with a bad fever." I dug the letter from my bundle and handed it to him.

He flicked it away. "Ye know I don't read. Mrs Reilly will read it when she comes back."

Michael thrust his chin at me. "Faith, Da, Katie can read right well."

Da looked at me. "That's right. Yer Mam did write that Granny Shea had been teaching ye. All right then, read me the news."

Suddenly my throat felt tight and froggy. I cleared it and read:

My dearest Seán,

First you must know our Patrick is not strong. The fever rages and burns in him. There is much fever here in our village. We do our best to keep Patrick cool and at rest and pray on our knees every night that the Lord will restore him to health. Patrick is sorely disappointed he couldn't make the journey to be with you." My cheeks flamed and my voice faded as I read, *"Katie helped with his care and will be a help to you in America. Father Shaughnessy says she is bright and it would be grand if she could go on with her learning . . ."*

Da's frown deepened. "What's that, Katie. I can't hear ye."

In a rush I said, "Mam says I should go on with my learning. She said that I'd be going to school here in America."

Da's face tightened. "School." He spat out the word. His

35

blue eyes bored into mine. "Ye mind what I say, Katie O'Brien. No child of mine will set foot in one of these schools. Full of propaganda they are." He ticked off his reasons, pounding his fist onto the arm of his chair for each one. "Make ye read the King James Bible," thump, "sing Protestant hymns," thump, "brainwash ye, turn ye into little Protestants," thump. "They're out to make ye forget yer Irish."

I felt my dream floating away. I had to catch it. "But, Da, Granny's friend used to write that her grandchildren went to school here. She said they learned so much . . . and, Da, I want to be a teacher . . . it's my dream . . ." My voice faltered as I watched Da's face.

He made a growly noise. "Yer dream is it? Well, 'tis time ye wake up and rid yerself of the highfalutin' ideas yer granny put in yer head. Here in America the only work for the Irish – if they can get past the 'Irish need not apply' signs – is low-paying and backbreaking. They'll take a few of us on to unload the cargo ships or dig ditches or scrub their floors." He made a disgusted sound. "Go on. Read the rest of the letter."

My hands trembled and I could feel hot blood rushing to my face. I would go to school! Somehow! I cleared my throat and gripped the letter tighter.

"Your brother Joseph and his dear wife Lily are sore pressed. We work like slaves as cottiers but have nothing to show for it. We await the next harvest, hoping the cold spring rain doesn't mean another bad crop. God willing, the potatoes never rot in the ground again. Joseph and Lily and our dear Patrick ask God's blessing for you. I sign myself your loving wife, Nora O'Brien."

Da's face softened. He stared into the lamplight. I wondered – was he picturing Mam and Patrick back home? Was he wishing them here instead of me? He rubbed his eyes.

When he opened them, he gave me a black look, then turned it on his foot. He slammed his fist and shouted so that I jumped. "And now this foot! The devil take Spike Wood and his gang. Know-Nothings, to be sure, taking their orders from the political big shots. 'Twas one of them let that barrel fall. If I hadn't been quick, 'twould have gotten more of me than my foot. But, I'll be back to work tomorrow. They'll not be rid of Seán O'Brien so easy."

Michael hitched his chair forward. "I can work, Da. I can take yer place till yer foot's better. Then maybe they'll take me on, too."

"Not much chance of that. Ye'll see nothing but 'Irish need not apply' signs."

Michael jumped to his feet. "I'll go back to Rooster. He said he could use a man like me."

Da's heavy brows rose high. "Rooster? Ye've met him?"

Michael told him what had happened – about the 'Go Back' signs, the attempted theft and the fight.

Da rubbed his face. "So, ye've had a go with Spike Wood's gang already.

"Who's Spike Wood?"

Da looked fierce. He pointed to his foot. "The man that did this. He's a loud-mouth Know-Nothing and a thug. Big Spike Wood they call 'im. Big Wood Head suits 'im better. Thick as a block of wood he is. The two ye met up with – the one ye call Weasel-face, and a weasel he is, is Frank Wood, Spike Wood's nephew. Yer Patch-eye's Butch Thompson, as mean as they come. That's how ye got that eye, huh?"

Michael nodded.

"Stay away from 'em. They're trouble." He fixed his eyes on Michael. His voice rose to a near shout. "But ye'll not work for Rooster. He's in heavy with the politicians. He'll be wanting ye for a ward worker – running errands and such – trying to get ye to sign on good Irishmen to become citizens – to give up their good Irish heritage. A traitor to Ireland he is!"

Mrs Reilly toed the door open and lugged in a good-smelling pot. She thumped it down on the stove, then turned and, hands on hips, scolded Da. "I could hear ye yelling out in the hall, Seán O'Brien. Don't be filling these children's minds with foolishness. The Irish that say we should get naturalized and get the right to vote are just following the bishop's advice. I read the Catholic paper to ye every week and ye know 'tis so." She glared at Da, then opened the firebox and roused the coals with the poker.

Da's face looked purple in the dim light. "Aggie Reilly, yer a good woman but a woman ye are. Ye know nothing at all about politics. This talk about getting the right to vote. What good will that do us? Give us a decent job? Not likely! They're out to take our heritage away, bishop or no!"

"Phew," Mrs Reilly spat out. She picked up an empty kettle and beckoned to me. "Katie, come along. I'll show ye where the water's at." She lit a candle stub and led me down the shadowy hall to the water tap. "Yer Da's a good man, but stubborn as a mule. Just won't listen to reason," she grumbled.

The wavering light showed mould creeping up the wall. Bugs scuttled by and I smelled a damp, musty odour. My skin crawling, I did as she bid me and filled the kettle with cold water. Together we hauled it back to Da's room.

"The Know-Nothings are just a bunch of blockheads," Da was saying to Michael. "Sneaky and sly. Close-lipped they are, keeping their dark ways secret."

Mrs Reilly put the kettle on to boil then took the bowls from the shelf and slammed them onto the table so hard I thought for sure they'd break. "They're not the only ones with secrets. We passed yer *friend*, Dennis O'Malley, on the way up. Recruiting more members for the United Irish, he was."

"Mind yer tongue, Aggie!"

"Ye know the Bishop is against those separatist Irish societies, Seán O'Brien, says their clannishness and bigotry will get the Irish nowhere. And I hear tell Dennis O'Malley's gang gets into a bit of violence."

"That's enough, Aggie Reilly!" Da thundered.

No one spoke. Soon the stew simmered and water boiled for tea.

Mrs Reilly poured the water over tea leaves. "Tea's ready."

Da groaned and his face went white as he stood to move his chair and the bucket. Dried blood stained the bandage round his foot. He look so tired. I moved quick to fix the bucket for him.

"I still say ye should have the doctor, Seán O'Brien," Mrs Reilly snapped.

"I've told ye, Aggie. I'll not be wasting good money on a doctor."

"Ye know the church would find free care for ye."

Da glowered. "I'll not take charity."

We sat round the scarred wood table and Mrs Reilly filled our bowls with steaming stew and placed a plate of bread in front of us. She sat down to join us. My mouth watered and my stomach rumbled. I couldn't remember the last time I'd seen such a spread. But my head was in such a spin my stomach felt queasy. I'd been right all along. Da didn't want me. Mrs Reilly hadn't even known I existed! And no school! If I could only go to school it wouldn't be so bad.

We ate in silence.

Da finished his stew and sat back. "Well, Michael,

tomorrow we'll leave early. I'll take ye to Lincoln's Wharf. We'll give it a try." He slurped his tea and ran his hand across his mouth. "Once in a while an Irish is in charge. Then some of us Irish get a chance to work."

Michael wiped his bowl with the last piece of bread. "Sure someone will take me on, Da."

Da turned to me. He scowled and his bristly brows drew into a single line. "And what will I do with ye?"

I looked down at my bowl, wishing I was back home with Mam and that Patrick was sitting here in my place.

Mrs Reilly set her cup down with a clatter. "I'll take her with me to the Pierce House tomorrow. Mr Pierce is a widower and leaves much of the running of the house to Mrs Plumley, the cook. She's needing more help and she's one of the few I know will take on an Irish. Says she's got such a hodge-podge of blood in her veins, she figures it don't matter what a person is. All she's interested in – is they do their work with spit and polish."

"Katie's a good worker," Michael said. "She helped with the farming back home."

Our eyes met and I smiled my thanks. Turning to Mrs Reilly, I asked, "What would I do there?"

"If Mrs Plumley sees fit to take ye on, ye'll be a servant girl-of-all-work. Ye'd help out in the kitchen and with the cleaning in Mr Pierce's grand house on Beacon Street."

"It's one of the places where Mrs Reilly does the wash," Da said. "For all her reading, that's the work she does – scrubs other people's dirty clothes."

"'Tis still good to read," Mrs Reilly snapped.

"But ye make yer money by the sweat of yer brow," Da said. He looked at me. "And if they take ye on, yer earnings will go towards bringing yer mam and yer brother, Patrick, over."

I nodded, liking the idea of helping with the fare. At least I agreed with Da on something!

Mrs Reilly said, "Ye'd be allowed a rest time every afternoon and a full afternoon off each week. Ye'd have room and board and near two dollars a month . . . if yer hired on."

My stomach lurched. "You mean – I'd live there? Michael and I wouldn't be together?"

7

The Pierce House

Early the next morning, Michael shook me awake. "Da and I are leaving now, Katie. Mrs Reilly will be by for ye soon."

I sat up so fast spots danced before my eyes. "Are you going then, Michael?"

"Aye, Katie."

"Hurry along, Michael." Da's voice came from the shadows near the sink. "Ye can make yerself a cup of tea, Katie, and there's a bite of bread." He limped over and stood above the pallet Michael and I had slept on. "I hope Mrs Reilly can find someone to take ye on."

My stomach jittered with nerves. "Sure and I'll find something, Da."

Da's lips tightened and he wiped the back of his hand across his forehead. "'Tis gonna be another scorcher of a day." He nudged Michael. "Come along, now."

Michael lifted his eyebrows and grinned at me, then leaned down and lightly kissed my forehead. He smelled of sweat and tea. "Good luck, little sister."

I smiled, feeling a bit better. "And to you, Michael." They

left and I was alone in the dim, stuffy room. The heavy odour of cooking oil seeped through the walls. I sat there, my hair and shift glued to me with sweat, and listened to the early morning noises of the building. Doors opening and shutting. Footsteps clattering down the stairs.

Something ran across my leg. I leapt to my feet. An enormous cockroach scurried away. Feeling itchy all over, I pulled on my stained dress, stepped into my shoes and took the bucket to the tap. Back in the room, I boiled water and poured it over tea leaves to steep, then added the rest to a bucket of cold water. I stripped naked and scrubbed myself raw with the warm water and a sliver of soap. At the sink, I poured a bowl of water over my hair and washed it best I could, then rubbed it dry with a ragged towel. I pulled my other shift and dress over my head. They were none too clean as the only washing we could do on board the ship was with icy sea water.

I poured a mug of tea and, though my stomach was in a jumble, forced down some bread. I pulled my wooden comb with the three missing teeth through my tangled hair. Though it was still damp, I plaited it in one long plait.

Mrs Reilly rapped on the door and pushed it open. "Are ye ready, Katie?"

"Aye, Mrs Reilly," I said.

Outside, the air felt wet though it wasn't raining. Mrs Reilly turned right and started up Hull Street. Silent men, heads bowed, walked down the hill. Heading to the wharf, I guessed. I thought of Michael with Da. Sure they would hire Michael, big and strong as he was. When would I see him again?

I rushed after Mrs Reilly's flying figure. Buildings rose on either side, blocking the sky, closing me in. I stopped and stared when Mrs Reilly climbed the steps to a graveyard. She turned and beckoned me with her head. "Ye can see Charlestown from up here. 'Tis the highest spot in the neighborhood – Copps Hill graveyard."

I clambered up after her. She pointed to a bridge far below. "That's the bridge to Charlestown – over the Charles River it goes. That's where I'll soon be managing a boarding house – all on my own." She sighed. "Had my Daniel lived long enough, we could've bought it outright, but there's those foolish laws against a woman owning property," she said in disgust.

I gazed at the river reflecting patches of early morning light and wondered if Da would ever be able to move from that dingy tenement. I'd help, I vowed. I'd work real hard and make him proud of me. Then Mam and Patrick would come over and we'd all move to Charlestown.

Mrs Reilly took a last look across the river and climbed down the steps at a brisk pace. I followed her through the twisting streets, trying to memorize their names. I trotted after her up Hanover to a bustling place called Scollay Square, filled with carriages, carts and people. Drivers shouted and cursed. Horses clip-clopped by, snorting and neighing. Pushcarts lined the pavements, offering vegetables, fruit, fish, foods of all kind! Women pointed to their choices and haggled about the prices. The noise was deafening. I stopped and gaped at everything. It was like nothing I'd ever seen before.

A street peddler cried. "Read the latest Peter Parley book! Learn about this great country of America."

I stopped. Books being sold right here on the street! A well-dressed woman picked up one of the books. I stood by her side looking at the pages as she turned them. Intrigued by the pictures, I moved closer.

The woman looked down at me. "You should keep the riffraff away if you want my business," she said to the peddler tossing the book back in the cart.

The man brought his hand back as though to cuff me. "Get on with ya. Ruining my business, the likes of ya are."

"Katie, over here," Mrs Reilly called from the other side of the street.

I ran into the road and a black two-seater drawn by a speedy horse nearly mowed me down. "Out of the way," the whip-wielding driver shouted.

Mrs Reilly grabbed my arm and pulled me along. "Best ye keep yer wits about ye, else ye'll be trampled."

"Mrs Reilly, that man was selling books. He had a whole cart of books!"

"Aye, but ye need money to buy one."

I pulled on her arm making her slow down. "Do you think, Mrs Reilly, I could go to school even if I'm a girl-of-all-work?"

"There'd not be time, Katie. And ye'd not disobey yer da, would ye? He's dead set against the public schools. Ye heard him last night."

"But . . ."

"But nothing, child. Hurry along now."

As we fled down Tremont Street, I wondered if there weren't some way I might go to school. They'd have books in the schools. Sure Da didn't want me to go because of all the – what did he call it? – propaganda, but I didn't have to listen to that. I'd study the books and learn all about the world. And I'd work, too. Sure there must be some way . . .

We passed two graveyards, King's Chapel and the Granary Burial Ground. I shivered despite the increasing heat. I'd hate to come by here at night, alone, I thought. I remembered stories I'd heard around the fire back home in Ireland, about the banshee – a spirit that wailed when death came for a loved one.

We passed a building with a shining gold dome. Mrs Reilly pointed to it. "That's the State House. A grand-looking building, 'tis." She crossed the road and turned into a park.

I raced after her then stopped, speechless. A field of grass, trees and flowers spread before me. "This is like the country!" I cried.

Mrs Reilly never slowed her stride. Throwing the words over her shoulder, she said, "This here's the Boston Common. Up ahead's the Public Garden. Open to anyone. Not just the rich folks."

We flew through the Common, then crossed Charles Street to the Public Garden. A cluster of rhododendrons, new blooms opening against dark green leaves, caught my eye. Beyond them a pond shimmered in the morning light. Wait till I tell Michael, I thought. This is just like home. We'll come here one day, we will.

We left the garden and found ourselves on Arlington Street, where narrow brownstone houses lined the walk. I stopped and stared at a sign in front of one of the houses. Big black letters shouted, *No Irish Need Apply*.

Mrs Reilly jabbed me with a sharp finger. "Ye'll see much of that, Katie. But I always say, 'Where there's a will there's a way'. Come along now. We're almost to the Pierce House." She scooted down an alley.

'Twixt and between hopeful and scared, I followed. Narrow courtyards on either side led to the back entrances of tall brown houses. At last, Mrs Reilly stepped into a small, walled courtyard lined with bricks. A shed leaned against the right wall. "Kitchen entrance," she explained, "for the likes of us and delivery men."

Mrs Reilly, her hand poised on the shed door, paused and looked at me. She pressed her thin lips together and shook her head. By now I was wet with perspiration. Curls had escaped the plait and hung before my eyes. I wiped my hands against my skirt and smoothed my hair. "Yer a sorry lookin' sight," she mumbled. "But a good uniform will spruce ye up a bit. If Mrs Plumley takes ye on, that is."

It was dark and cool inside the shed. Mrs Reilly pushed open another door and stepped into the kitchen. "Wait here, Katie, I've got the wash to start. I hope Peg's got the coals heatin' under the tub." She left the kitchen.

I looked around. I'd never seen such a fine kitchen. It was spotless. A copper sink and a coal stove, glowing with heat, were against the left wall, and a big table, loaded with trays and crockery, stood in the middle of the room. Another table, covered with a red patterned cloth, stood against the light-green wall to the right of the door that Mrs Reilly had disappeared through. Wouldn't Mam love these? I thought, going to the centre table and picking up a blue and white plate to study its design.

"Put that down, you little thief."

Startled, I dropped the plate and it smashed into pieces. Horrified, I stared at it, then at the woman. Near tall as Da, she stood there with her hands jammed against the waist of her dark blue dress. She stared back from close-set, dark eyes.

Fire burned my cheeks. "Faith, I'm not a thief, Mrs Plumley. I'm Katie O'Brien, come for a position. Mrs Reilly said . . ."

The tall woman's nostrils flared. She stepped closer to me and I nearly choked from her heavy perfume. In a clipped

English accent that made me feel small as a toad, she said, "A Paddy right off the boat! Ignorant girl! Do I look like a cook? I'm Miss Pratt, the governess." She frowned. "Don't stare. Don't you know to keep your eyes lowered when addressing your betters?"

Just then a short woman waddled into the room. "Lord's sake! Who broke that plate?"

"This little Paddy – right off the boat. I'll leave her to you." Miss Pratt sniffed. She patted the curly bangs fringing her forehead and smoothed the sides of her upswept chestnut hair. "I came down to see if Miss Elizabeth was here. You know she's to stay above stairs."

Mrs Plumley pulled her plump self up. "The child's not been down this morning."

"Very well." Miss Pratt swept from the kitchen, her flounced blue skirt swaying. I could hear the solid thud of her footsteps going up a flight of stairs off the hallway.

Mrs Plumley folded her hands on the ledge of her stomach, tapped her forefingers together and stared at me. She was all circles – round cheeks, round chins, a round bosom and a great round stomach.

Mrs Reilly, hands dripping suds, and a bony girl about my age, lost in the folds of a dark dress with a white apron over it, crowded into the room. "Ach, Katie O'Brien, yer off to a good start, ye are," said Mrs Reilly, surveying the mess on the floor and wringing her bony, large knuckled hands.

"So, Mrs Reilly, who is this young'un?"

"'Tis Katie O'Brien. I knew ye were looking for a girl to help out. Katie just got here yesterday and needs the work. I brought her by for ye to talk to."

Mrs Plumley stared at me, then at Mrs Reilly. "We'll talk about it while you're sorting laundry." The women started from the kitchen.

My heart kicked out in my chest. What if she said no? I stepped over the broken plate. "Mrs Plumley, please ma'am," I cried. She stopped and looked over her plump shoulder at me. "I'm a very good worker. I'm sorry about the plate. It was an accident. I'll work very hard. I will!"

She squinted at me, then said to the skinny girl carrying a big bowl from the pantry, "Peg Callahan, you get on with the breakfast chores, and you – Katie is it? You clean up that mess." She and Mrs Reilly, talking in low murmurs, left the kitchen.

"Here, let me help," Peg said. She put the bowl on the centre table and went to the shed, bringing in a broom and dustpan. Limp blonde hair straggled out from beneath her white cap. Dark circles shadowed her pale blue eyes. She was so thin and her pale skin stretched so tight across her cheekbones, I near could see through it. She swept the broken pottery into the dustpan I held in place. "You dump it in the trash," she said. "There's a basket in the shed."

When I came back into the kitchen, Peg had set a steaming, milky mug of tea on the table. "Sit there and take a sip," she said. "Yer looking right peaked."

I hesitated and swallowed tears that clogged my throat. "What will Mrs Plumley think if I'm sitting here drinking tea when she comes back?"

"Um, I tell you what. You pare the potatoes at the sink there. Ye can sip the tea while you're working."

I smiled my thanks and went to the sink, glad to busy my hands with a chore for they were trembling with worry.

Peg went into the pantry and returned with an apron full of eggs. She set them on the table, then, briskly breaking them into the bowl, said, "Ye just come over from Ireland, did ye?"

"Aye. I'm hoping Mrs Plumley takes me on. I want to help pay for my Mam's and brother's passage over."

"Your Mam's living, and ye've a brother, too?" Peg sighed. "I lost the last of my family to lung sickness two years gone."

Mrs Plumley shuffled into the kitchen. "Well, Katie O'Brien, Mrs Reilly recommends you, but . . . I don't know . . ."

The tea swished and gurgled in my stomach so loud I thought she might hear it. "You won't be sorry if you take me on, Mrs Plumley. I promise."

"I'm willing to give you a try . . . for a month. Of course, that plate would come out of your wages."

I felt weak with relief. "Thank you, ma'am," I said.

"Not so fast. I'm willing, but I have to clear it with Mr Pierce. Come by tomorrow and I'll tell you for sure then."

8

Back to the Waterfront

Mrs Reilly and I stood in a wedge of shade by the courtyard shed. She rubbed her long nose till it shone bright red, then slapped her hands on her hips. "Well, yer as good as in, Katie. 'Tis really up to Mrs Plumley. 'Tis just form, checking with Mr Pierce. Now I've work to do – here and at other houses. Best ye just wait here in the courtyard, then on with me to the next place. I've not the time to take ye back to yer da's."

"Sure I can find my way to the waterfront, Mrs Reilly! Then I'll go to Lincoln's Wharf where my da and Michael will be."

Mrs Reilly shook her head. "Best ye stay with me. Ye might get lost. Then what would I tell yer da!"

"But I can ask the way to the waterfront. I'll just go on back through that park and . . ."

"Mrs Reilly, the water's boiling and there's wash needs doing," Mrs Plumley called from the door.

Mrs Reilly frowned at me, then cried to Mrs Plumley, "I'm coming! I'm coming!"

I headed for the alley and said over my shoulder, "Sure and go on, Mrs Reilly. I'll be fine."

51

I was itching to go through the parks and back into Boston's streets. A whole day to explore on my own! First I'd find a peddler selling books, then look for Michael.

Mrs Reilly nodded and hurried back into the house. I walked down the alley, light as air. Through the Common and onto Tremont Street. Back in Scollay Square I looked for a peddler selling books but couldn't find one. In a narrow by-way, I passed a warehouse. A sign reading *Grammar School* was stuck in a window. My heart jumped. A school right here in front of me.

The three-story building looked like a stiff wind would blow it over. The front door leaned open. I walked up two wooden steps and stood there picking at a chip of paint. I took a deep breath and stepped inside. On either side of a stuffy hallway, doors opened into rooms filled with crates and barrels. Men were unloading more crates from a handcart. Dust tickled my nose and I sneezed and sneezed.

A familiar voice behind me said, "Good day, Miss Katie O'Brien. And what brings you to this particular building? I'd hazard a guess 'tis the sign that proclaims it a school." Mr O'Donnell smiled down at me.

I grinned so wide I thought my cheeks would crack. "Sure, Mr O'Donnell, 'tis good to see you."

He shifted the weight of his black bag and beckoned me to follow him up the rickety stairs. "The school room, I'm told, is on the second floor. Closed this time of year."

The higher we climbed the staler the air grew. Mr O'Donnell pushed at a stuck door that finally gave with a groan. A sour smell rushed out. Rows of desks and chairs, some broken, filled the dim, dusty room. Noise from the street drummed against the dirty windows. I pictured the room full of children, myself at a desk and a master, someone just like Mr

O'Donnell, at the big desk in front. He would read to us from great books. We'd learn all about America and the land that stretched west. And numbers! We'd learn . . .

"So, Katie. I would guess that you are dreaming yourself into a student. Would that I could teach a group as hungry for knowledge as yourself." Mr O'Donnell sat on the edge of a table and looked about the room.

"Oh, sure it would be grand if you could be a master! Are you asking round about it?"

"No need to ask, Katie. There's no chance of me, an Irish, being hired on. That is what Rooster and all the 'Irish Need Not Apply" signs tell me."

"But you should try, Mr O'Donnell! Sure and didn't you tell me not to give up my dream?"

"Aye, Katie. But first things first. Man needs to eat. I shall accept Rooster's offer of employment."

"What will you do?"

"I will become a politician. I will knock on doors and try to persuade the men of Ward One to become involved in their new country."

I sat at one of the desks and scratched my head. "What's a ward?"

"A district. A territory. Boston's north end, which is where your da lives, is part of Ward One. 'Tis those who live there that Rooster and his workers hope will become naturalized citizens."

"Why? What's so important about that?"

Mr O'Donnell pointed a long finger at me. "Because then a man has the right to vote. And 'tis voting that will get the man he wants to represent him into office."

"That's what Mrs Reilly, the lady who met us, says. My da says 'tisn't so. He says we have to keep our heritage."

Mr O'Donnell leaned forward. "Becoming an American citizen does not mean your father would lose his heritage. The two are not opposite sides of a coin. Your Mrs Reilly is right. Has it not been said that 'The pen is mightier than the . . ."

I laughed, remembering the quote from talks we'd had on the ship. "I know, 'The pen is mightier than the sword.'"

We clattered down the stairs, Mr O'Donnell lugging his satchel. We stepped out into the blistering heat, a heat nothing like we ever had in Ireland.

Mr O'Donnell pulled out his handkerchief and wiped his face. "What are your plans for the rest of this day, Katie?"

"I'm going down to the waterfront to see if I can find Michael."

"And I to see Rooster."

He fell into step beside me. As we walked, I told him about my morning, and we decided that after he talked with Rooster, we would look for Michael together. In a narrow alley, we passed a stable reeking of horse manure. A rat big as a cat ran by. Soon, we were on the noisy, bustling waterfront, so familiar now I couldn't believe I'd arrived just yesterday. I stopped to gaze at a vendor's cart full of books.

"I see you are wanting a book, Katie. Would that I could afford to buy one from that sweaty gentlemen, who's more interested in the pennies he pockets than the books he peddles. But since I cannot, I will share my meagre library with you." Mr O'Donnell crouched down and opened his black satchel, searched through the contents and handed me The Adventures of Ulysses by Charles and Mary Lamb.

"It is the story of Odysseus. He journeyed for ten years experiencing many adventures before returning home."

I smoothed my hand over the book's worn cover. "Oh,

thank you, Mr O'Donnell. I'll take very good care of it. I promise."

Mr O'Donnell smiled. "I know you will, Katie."

We threaded out way through the crowd to *Rooster's Grog Shop*.

"You wait here, Katie. I'll be out shortly," Mr O'Donnell said, pushing the door open. The smell of a meat stew wafted out making my stomach rumble and growl. I sat on an overturned barrel and pulled The Adventures of Ulysses from my pocket. I opened the worn book carefully. But there was so much going on I couldn't concentrate. Men kept going in and out of Rooster's. Someone left the door open. I edged closer and peeked in.

The room was full of tables and wooden chairs and smelled of beer. Sawdust covered the floor. Some men played cards. Others talked in low voices. Most all of them had a pint and a bowl of food. It smelled so good!

Mr O'Donnell was talking to Rooster. He took a packet of papers from him and slipped them into his bag. He caught sight of me and winked. I watched him walk to a table of food. A sign over the table read, *Free Lunch with a 5 cent Beer*. He filled two bowls with stew.

I pulled over another barrel for him. He handed me the steaming hot dish. My mouth was watering buckets. I spooned in a tender piece of meat and thick brown gravy. Rich flavours filled my mouth. The big, dark green pickle surprised me with a spicy sourness that made my eyes water. I bit into a crusty chunk of bread spread with butter. Real butter. A feast! I thought of the scant food, some of it spoiled, on the ship. America was truly a great country. And such good food.

The noise around us grew louder. Men separated from the

passing crowd and collected round a speaker. He stood on a makeshift platform – a wide board balanced on two overturned crates. Mr O'Donnell and I finished our meal, then, curious, joined the group.

A short man – his round head bobbing on his skinny neck, waved his fist in the air. "America, my friends, is for Americans. Why should this country suffer this massive influx of Irish? Because Boston is the closest port to Ireland, is it fair that they come here in droves?"

I looked up at the gathering men. Their faces looked hot and angry. Uneasiness trembled through me.

The short man went on. "These foreigners come to reap the benefit of what we Americans have worked so hard to achieve. These immigrants are the dregs of society. Slaves to religious despotism. For don't they pledge their loyalty to a foreign prince – the pope? How then, can they be loyal to our United States of America?" He thrust his scrawny neck out of his stiff collar and swept the growing crowd with bulging eyes.

Voices called out:

"We'd have work if they weren't here."

"They're spreading disease. My wife's down with a sickness now."

"America for Americans!" one man cried.

Others took up the chant.

Swarthy, sweat-smelling men swarmed round me. Some were using signs to bully their way front. I saw the words, *Irish – Go Home*. Everything went quiet inside me. There were Know-Nothings in this group!

I yanked on Mr O'Donnell's arm. My throat dry, I croaked, "Mr O'Donnell, let's . . ."

He shoved his bag at my feet. "Katie, watch this for me." He starting elbowing his way through the crush.

Chills prickled my neck and raced down my spine.

I caught glimpses of the platform through shifting heads. The short man, his face purple, mopped his brow with a handkerchief. Just as he opened his mouth like a fish, Mr O'Donnell leapt up onto the platform. He towered over the shorter man. A stunned silence followed.

A hard fist of fear cramped my stomach. What was Mr O'Donnell doing?

He jabbed a slender finger at a man in the crowd. "You there. Where did your parents hail from?"

The man stared at him, open-mouthed, then, pulling his shoulders back, shouted, "Born here, they were. Right here in the United States of America."

Mr O'Donnell's eyes riveted the man. "And your grandparents – on your mother's side?"

"Why . . . why . . . I reckon they came from Germany."

"And on your father's side?"

The man's colour deepened. "Germany, too. But my parents – both of 'em were born right here."

Mr O'Donnell said nothing. Then, making eye-contact with men in the swelling crowd, he said in a low, but carrying voice, "How many of you have two parents born in America?"

His voice rose. "And if not two parents, two grandparents?"

He waited.

A simmering stillness filled the blazing heat. Then men started shuffling feet and muttering.

Mr O'Donnell's voice grew louder. "How far back can any of you go without acknowledging an immigrant in your family?"

A few men looked shamefaced.

Most buzzed angrily.

The angry buzz grew louder. Men exchanged looks. They

were passing signals! My heart jumped and pounded against my ribs.

Mr O'Donnell's rich voice went on. "Does not every man have the right to emigrate from one country to another? Did not the first settlers of this country come to escape oppression? Are you not all descendants of foreigners?"

Someone shouted, "My heritage is good English stock."

Movement and whispers behind me. I turned round. Men were trickling from the group, then running to an alley and returning with buckets and pails. Weasel-face! There he was, lugging two pails, scurrying like a rat toward the crowd.

The reek of rubbish reached me. Icy cold, I froze to the spot. Michael! Da! Where were they? Were they all right?

A huge man, hairy as an ape, shouted, "This country's for native-born Americans! Native born, I say."

Other voices cried out:

"Native born!"

"Send the immigrants back."

The short man on the platform, his Adam's apple bobbing in his rubber neck, shoved Mr O'Donnell aside and popped in front of him. "The first men to come to this country were honourable, upright men," he bleated. "Now the dregs of society – drunks, thieves, beggars fill our streets . . .".

Mr O'Donnell raised both arms, his outspread hands asking for quiet. "There is room in this great country for . . ."

The giant man, his dull black hair plastered against his red face, waved his hairy arms, big as clubs, and shouted, "Who are you to . . ."

Weasel-face tugged on his arm. The huge man bent his head to him. With a roar, he thundered, "Just here yesterday, are ya? And already telling us what to do! Go back to where ya came from. It's you Micks taking the jobs."

He swung his immense head from side to side. "There's a Mick in charge down at Lincoln's Wharf today. It's a Mick saying who'll work the ships. And what does that Mick do? He gives the other Micks work. Taking the bread right out of our mouths, they are." He took something from Weasel-face's pail and flung it at Mr O'Donnell.

An egg burst open on Mr O'Donnell's forehead. Its stickiness dripped into his eyes, ran down his cheeks and clogged his brown whiskers.

Weasel-face and the other men hustled through the crowd passing the pails of slops. Man after man pelted Mr O'Donnell with handfuls of swill.

Weasel-face stopped dead when he saw me. "You! You were with 'em yesterday. Little snot-nose Irish."

Unable to move, I stared at his bruised mouth and his broken rotted teeth. His eyes, close-set in his thin, sallow face, narrowed. He reached out and drew his dirty hand down the side of my face, down my neck, then grasped my shoulder.

My mouth dry and my heart hammering, I pulled back. His fingers dug through the thin material of my dress into my flesh.

"You'll go when I let you go, little snot-nose Irish," he sneered.

I struggled to free myself but he grabbed my other shoulder and held me tight. He leaned close, breathing his foul breath into my face. "What's your name, cutie? And what's that big guy's name, your brother was it, your big protective brother? Well, he's not here now, is he?"

I squirmed under his cruel hands and turned my face from his. He grabbed my chin and forced me to look at him. His words fast and distorted, spittle spurting from his mouth, he

59

threatened, "You tell that Mick that Franky Wood's out to get 'im. That Franky Wood's gonna find out who he is. Then he'd better watch his back 'cause he's gonna pay for knocking my teeth out! And you . . ."

Oh, where was Mr O'Donnell? Why didn't he come back?

"You," he leered. "I'll take care of you, too, but for now . . ." Like lightning, he squashed a handful of slimy slops in my face. "Tell me his name, cutie."

Bile burned my throat. Tears stung my eyes, Choking. Gagging. I spit out the offal.

Suddenly the giant loomed over us.

Weasel-face shouted above the racket of the screaming crowd. "Big Spike. She was with those guys yesterday – the ones did this to me." He pointed to his mouth. "She's one of 'em."

Big Spike Wood glared down at me. A swollen vein throbbed and pulsed on his temple. His eyes, a dead-black, reflected no light – only hatred.

A cold hand strangled my heart and I began to tremble. This is the man who hurt Da. He hurt Da.

"Lookee here," Weasel-face crowed, pulling Mr O'Donnell's papers from his bag. "Looks like the old man's trying to make citizens out of the rabble."

Spike Wood grabbed the packet. Muttering. "Foreign pigs. No good paupers," he ripped the papers and threw them high.

The hot crowd pressed closer. Weasel-face held up a book, squinted inside it. He mouthed, "Séamus O'Donnell," he gloated, "so that's the old guys name – Séamus O'Donnell." He broke the book's binding; laughing, tore its pages. He tossed books to others. They shredded and trampled them.

Through the racket, I heard Mr O'Donnell crying, "Katie! Katie!"

I wiped my hand across my mouth, scrunched down and snatched a book. Weasel-face kicked. His heavy boot struck my hand. Sharp pains shot up my arm.

Mr O'Donnell, splotched with rubbish, pushed past the men. He pulled me to my feet. "Come, Katie!"

"Your books! Your books!" I cried.

"Move, Katie! Now!" His hand tightened on my arm, dragging me along.

We ran.

The screaming mob followed. Eggs and fistfuls of wet gooey mess rained upon us as we sped down the waterfront.

9

An Afternoon at the Pierce House

A fierce August sun streamed through the window and turned the kitchen into an oven. Sweat beaded my forehead. I picked up a hot iron from the stove and set the cool one to heat. I pressed the heavy iron to the linen tablecloth. The damp fabric hissed and starchy steam bathed my face.

Mrs Plumley wiped her hands on her apron. She sighed heavily, then waddled over to check my work. "Too many wrinkles, Katie. Keep that linen moist and the iron spittin'. Lord's sake! You've been here three weeks now. I shouldn't have to be tellin' you every little thing." She pressed a wet cloth to her fiery face. "This heat. It's hotter than Hades. Now where's Peg got to? I want her to peel vegetables."

"I'm right here, Mrs Plumley. I just took the breakfast slops out," Peg said, coming through the door, strands of pale hair stuck to her forehead.

"You best get started on the vegetables. Mr. Pierce said there'll be six extra tonight. I'm off for me lie-down. Me feet are killin' me." She shuffled toward the stairs to climb to the servants' quarters on the fifth floor, then turned and wagged her finger at me. "And you be careful with those frills on Miss Elizabeth's dresses."

"Yes, Mrs Plumley."

She grunted and shambled into the hall. "Lord's sake! How do I ever manage with the likes of you two?"

Peg looked at me and grinned. "By the time she gets to the attics she'll be real winded."

I wiped my forehead. Sweat pasted my hair to my temples. "Maybe it will keep her from telling us what to do every second," I said. I pulled my uniform, a dark blue cotton dress covered with a white apron, away from my skin to let in puffs of air. Oh to be sitting on my rock by the lough now, a cool breeze blowing across the water.

Peg snorted. "Never. I've . . ." a fit of coughing stopped her. When she caught her breath, she went on, "I've been here near two years now and Mrs Plumley can always find breath to tell you what to do." She darted a look at me. "And how're things with Michael?"

Peg's pale face flushed. I hid a smile. Peg was smitten with Michael. Mrs Plumley had hired him on for the odd job – filling the coal bin and such. We had Mrs Reilly to thank for that. She'd done the same for Michael at other houses. But those odd jobs were few and far between.

When he was here, he sang as he worked and Peg loved to listen to him. She'd sigh over the quiet tunes and laugh over the jolly ones. I wondered how Michael could always be singing, what with all the worry on his mind.

I shook my head. "Faith, Peg, he's had no luck finding steady work. And that Weasel-face . . ." I shuddered, feeling again his rough hands and the splat of slops in my face.

Peg frowned. "Has he been after Michael again, then?"

"He and some other thugs jumped him in an alley. I fear

what would have happened if Mr. O'Donnell and some other men hadn't come along." My stomach tightened at the thought. "Michael says he's not afraid of Weasel-face, that he's a coward. But then, he's always got others, just like himself, with him. There's no telling what they'll do!" A cold chill crept through me, remembering that day on the waterfront. There'd been so much hatred in the air. And Weasel-face and Spike Wood – I shivered though the heat in the kitchen was fierce – they hated me. Their hatred had burned me that day and I prayed God I'd never see them again.

The precise step of Thomas, the butler, sounded on the stairs. He walked through hallway to the kitchen. Standing erect, every strand of his steel-grey hair in place, he looked at us with his protruding pale eyes. With an angry spot of color on either cheek, he said, "Miss Pratt sent me to inquire why no one has answered her bell." He took a deep breath and his mouth tightened. In measured words, he continued, "I discovered the bell-cord to the music room was in a tangle, which I have corrected."

Just then the bell jangled. "Oh, dear," Peg cried, drying her hands and starting from the kitchen. "I'll see what she wants."

Thomas tilted his head to the side and held up a hand to stop her. "That won't be necessary. She would like two glasses of cold lemonade, one for her and one for Miss Elizabeth." He left the kitchen, muttering, "That woman, treating me like I'm her personal servant."

Peg rushed to the icebox in the shed for the lemonade while I set a doily and two glasses on a tray. She hurried back with the pitcher and filled the glasses. "That Miss Pratt! She sets my nerves on edge."

"'*Pratt the rat's* a good name for her," I mumbled.

Peg, holding the pitcher, looked at me with wide eyes. "Ach, don't let her hear you say that! Ye'd be sacked for sure." Then, suddenly, she broke into giggles. "*Pratt the rat!* Oh, Katie, you're a howl, ye are!"

I grinned. It was good to hear Peg laugh. I put a few cookies on a plate and placed it on the tray. "Do you mean the rat could get me sacked? I thought Mrs Plumley was in charge."

Peg pursed her lips and shook her head. "She used to be, but now with Miss Pratt here, I don't think Mrs Plumley's so sure of herself. And Miss Pratt . . ." she hesitated. Lowering her voice she said, "Ye know, Katie, she fought against you being taken on. Thomas heard her tell Mr Pierce there's many girls from good English stock looking for work. 'Why take on an ignorant Irish immigrant?' she said."

"But he did take me on. So he listened to Mrs Plumley."

"Aye. This time. But Mrs Plumley and Thomas – both of 'em – are worried that Miss Pratt's worming her way into Mr Pierce's good graces. And her here only seven months now."

"I thought she'd been here since Elizabeth's mother died."

"No, old Mrs Mason was here then. And sure Miss Elizabeth was happier then." She snorted. "We were all happier before Miss Pratt. Before she came, Mr Pierce consulted with Mrs Plumley and Thomas about dinner parties and such. Now it's, 'What does Miss Pratt think?'"

The bell pealed again. "I'd better take this up." Her voice fell to a whisper. "To *Pratt the rat*." Laughing, she left the kitchen.

I was glad Peg had taken the tray to Miss Pratt. She made me edgy, always looking to find something wrong. I sprinkled more water on the heavy cloth and picked up the iron. My thoughts went back to Michael and Da. Both of them down on the waterfront every day, never knowing what Spike Wood or Weasel-face might do. And all the other Know-Nothings! And Mr. O'Donnell, too. Him going round giving speeches, passing out those papers. Something was bound to happen.

"Ach, Katie, mind what you're doing! Don't be scorching that cloth," Peg said, coming into the kitchen. She went to the sink and starting shelling peas. They fell into the bowl with little plinks. "That woman," Peg muttered. "Miss Elizabeth always looks like a sorrowful pup when she's with her. In truth, I hope Mrs Plumley and Thomas aren't right about her settin' her cap for Mr Pierce."

"What? Miss Pratt wanting to marry Mr Pierce?"

"Aye. And she wouldn't be the first governess coming over from England hoping to marry above herself. What with Mr Pierce being a widower and needing a wife to run the household and someone to care for Miss Elizabeth . . . Mrs Plumley says Miss Pratt's got her eye on the money. She says, 'God help the child if Miss Pratt wins him.' I say, God help us all if *Pratt the rat* comes to be mistress of this house." She tossed a handful of peas into the bowl, then leaning against the sink, gazed out the window. "Ah, Katie, how I'd like to get up in the world. I'm not wanting to be a hired girl all my life."

"What do you want to be, Peg?" I asked, rubbing my stiff neck.

"Oh," she said dreamily, "maybe a shop girl. Dress up in pretty clothes and work in one of them big stores, maybe one that Mr Pierce owns. He has three stores here in Boston, ye know, and one in New York. Thomas says he has merchandise coming into port from all over the world. If I worked in one of those stores . . ." Peg straightened her shoulders, smiled and bowed her head slightly, "I'd say to the customers, 'Can I help you, ma'am?'" She sighed and turned back to the sink. "'Course, I need to get some learning. But how can I get any schooling? I've no one to help me, my family being all gone to the Great Beyond."

"My good friend Mr. O'Donnell? He says you can learn without going to school. That reading will open other worlds to you."

Peg snorted. "That's all well and good, but first ye must know your letters."

"But, Peg, I'll teach you your letters. Then you could learn to read and . . ."

Light footsteps flew down the stairs and seven-year-old Elizabeth Pierce burst into the room. Brown eyes glowing, she said. "Miss Pratt's taking her rest."

Peg stiffened and got all quiet. She liked Elizabeth but was uneasy with the routine Elizabeth and I had. She said I'd get in trouble for sure. That Miss Pratt would say I was trying to move in on her territory. Elizabeth had light brown curls and dark brown eyes. She had beautiful clothes and her own pony. She had everything a girl could want, except her mam.

The first time I'd met her, we'd felt a special friendship. She had sneaked down to the kitchen to see the "feeble-minded '*imbasilly*'" that Miss Pratt said had been hired on. I'd laughed and laughed and Elizabeth, not knowing why, had laughed, too.

"Are there any cookies or cake?" Elizabeth asked.

"Miss Elizabeth, you just had a glass of lemonade," Peg said.

Elizabeth pouted. "I didn't like it. It was sour. Anyway, food tastes better here in the kitchen with Katie."

I plonked the iron on the stove and headed for the butler's pantry. Peg picked up a carrot and pared it furiously. "Don't take too much, Katie. If anything's missing, Mrs Plumley will be at us."

I sliced a small piece of chocolate cake and put it on a plate, then went to the shed for ice. I loved the icebox. Cold food right at your fingertips! I opened the upper cabinet and chipped some ice from the block. I rubbed the slivers across my face.

"Oh, let me," Elizabeth pleaded, reaching for the ice pick.

"No! That's dangerous," I said. I took the pick and chipped some for her.

She held the pieces against her rosy cheeks. "Oh, it's shivery," she said with a little shudder.

I brought some chips to Peg. She popped a few in her mouth, then rubbed the rest on the back of her neck. I went back to the shed and poured a glass of milk for Elizabeth. She sat at the center table eating the cake and drinking the cold milk. My mouth watered as I watched her. Mrs Plumley kept strict track of the food. 'I don't want to be findin' anything missin'. Mr Pierce provides plenty for us and I have to answer to him for the provisions,' she'd say, her hands folded on her stomach ledge and her forefingers beating against each other.

Elizabeth finished her cake. Peg washed, dried, and put the dishes away, then rinsed potatoes to peel. Elizabeth jumped up from the table and came to watch me. "I like the smell," she said, sniffing the hot, starchy smell rising from the board. She stood watching, twisting one of her curls. "Let me try, Katie."

"The iron's too heavy for you, Elizabeth," I said, placing the cooled iron on the stove. I folded the tablecloth and went to the pantry to store it among the linens.

"Is it your rest time yet?" she asked, eyes wide and hopeful.

I grinned, "Aye, 'tis time for a rest. Shall I read you one of the Grimm's stories today?"

Elizabeth skipped to the pantry to get the book we kept hidden there. "Read 'The Ash Maiden'. I love that story. It's my very favourite."

As we left the kitchen, I caught Peg's disapproving look. She'd promised to keep an ear for Miss Pratt or Mrs Plumley when I read to Elizabeth. I'd been reading to Elizabeth on my rest time for the best part of two weeks now, and everyday Peg warned me, 'Sure and you're headed for trouble.'

Outside, one tree grew in the little courtyard. Its branches were low and heavy with leaves. We settled under it and leaned against its broad trunk. A warm earth scent stole from the ground like perfume and mixed with Elizabeth's light lavender scent. I opened Elizabeth's beautiful copy of Grimm's Fairy Tales. She leaned against my shoulder as I began 'The Ash Maiden".

"One more, Katie. One more story," Elizabeth pleaded when I finished.

I scooted from beneath the tree and stretched, then shook my skirts loose from where they'd stuck to my legs. "I can't, Elizabeth. I've the ironing to finish."

Elizabeth dashed by me in the shed. I chipped more ice for us and followed her into the kitchen. Elizabeth grabbed a hot iron from the stove and pressed it against a lace-trimmed petticoat. "Oh," she wailed as the smell of scorched cotton filled the room, "I've burned my petticoat."

My stomach plunged. I yanked the iron off the burning cloth.

Peg, hands dripping water, gazed at the brown spot and the melted lace trim. She looked up at me, horrified. "Ye'll be sacked for sure, Katie."

10

Trouble

I stared at the scorched petticoat. "I can't get sacked, Peg," I said, my voice cracking. "My da's counting on my earnings."

Elizabeth twisted a curl round a finger and sobbed. "But I did it."

"Aye, but you're not supposed to be workin'. If Miss Pratt knew that . . ." Peg shook her head and rolled her eyes. "Katie will get in deep for sure. Ye know how Miss Pratt faults her."

Elizabeth snatched the scorched petticoat. "Nobody need know, Peg. I'll hide it in my dresser." She stepped into the petticoat and pulled it up over her knickerbockers. Plucking at the waist of her light blue dress to straighten the bunched fabric, she said, "I'm sorry . . . I just wanted to do something."

"Ironing's not what you should be doing, Miss Elizabeth," Peg scolded.

Elizabeth frowned and chewed on her lower lip. Suddenly she dashed from the room. Peg and I stared at each other as we listened to her clatter up the stairs.

"Maybe no one will find out," Peg said.

My hand shook as I picked up an iron. "Oh, Peg, I hope not."

A few minutes later, Elizabeth flew back to the kitchen holding a book and some paper. She spread the book open on the table, and placed the paper and pencil next to it. "I'll do my lessons here," she announced.

Peg shook her head. "Faith, Miss Elizabeth, you'll be caught down here sure as shootin'. You know Miss Pratt thinks you're doing your lessons in the music room, then resting in your bedroom when she's on her free time."

Elizabeth bent her head lower over her book. "I like it here. It's lonesome upstairs."

Peg opened her eyes wide at me as though to say, "What should we do?"

I looked away. I liked Elizabeth in the kitchen with us. I sniffed the air, inhaling the smell of burnt cotton. It just had to clear before Mrs Plumley came down. I watched Elizabeth study her book, then write numbers on her paper. Out of the corner of my eye, I saw Peg watching too.

I finished one of Mr Pierce's shirts and rubbed my aching shoulders, then went to peek over Elizabeth's shoulder. "Ah, you're learning sums, Elizabeth. Would that I could go to school and study numbers."

Elizabeth, open-mouthed and wide-eyed, stared at me. "You mean you *want* to go to school?"

"Faith, Elizabeth, I do! If I don't get learning I'll be a hired girl all my life."

"Aye," Peg said sadly. "That's what I'll be. I've no chance of schooling."

Elizabeth twisted her pencil round and round then said wistfully, "I wish we could all go to school together. It would be a lot more fun than having lessons all alone with Miss Pratt." She jumped from her chair and clapped her hands. "We could have our own school right here in the kitchen."

Peg snorted. "We've work to do, Miss Elizabeth."

"We could do it on your free time, Peg. I'll share my books with you and tell you what Miss Pratt tells me. I'll pay close attention so I get it right."

Firm steps sounded on the stairs and Miss Pratt marched into the kitchen. "Elizabeth, what are you doing down here?" she snapped.

Elizabeth bit her bottom lip and frowned. She nodded at her books. "My sums, Miss Pratt." She took a deep breath, then, all in a rush, blurted, "I thought I'd share my books with Katie and Peg. We could all study here in the kitchen."

Miss Pratt's angry, close-set eyes flew from Peg to me. "Ridiculous! Come upstairs at once. The kitchen's no place for you."

Elizabeth frowned. "But Katie doesn't want to be a hired girl all her life and if she doesn't . . ."

Miss Pratt's jaw fell open. A bright red spot appeared on either cheek. "Oh, so the little Paddy doesn't want to be a hired girl? So she asks you to teach her your lessons? Upstairs with you! Right now!" Nostrils flaring, she sniffed the air, "What is that awful smell?"

Elizabeth flashed me a look. "I don't smell anything," she said, gathering up her books. "I'll go upstairs now, but I'm going to ask Papa about the lessons. And it wasn't Katie's idea. It was mine. But Katie says it's important to learn."

Miss Pratt scowled at me. "I don't care what Katie says. I will be talking to your father myself, and I will tell him about Katie O'Brien and her uppity ideas. I had no problem with you before *she* came." She wrinkled her nose and sniffed the air once more, then, prodding Elizabeth before her, swept out of the room.

11

Wind of Change

A huge sailor held Maggie's shrouded body over the rails of a ship. "Does anyone want to say a prayer . . . say a prayer . . . say a prayer?" he intoned. His voice rattled into a cough. The sailor faded into Spike Wood. He lifted the oblong bundle. Weasel-face stepped forward. Mocking the sign of the cross he chanted, "No priest. No priest. No priest . . ." NO, I tried to shout, but could make no sound. NO, I cried, struggling to move forward – wanting to hold Maggie, warm and living, in my arms. The rattling cough grew louder and louder. Big Spike loomed taller, thinner. His face melted into Miss Pratt's. She sniffed the air. "What is that smell? Lessons? You? Ha ha ha!" She tossed Maggie's little body and it tumbled down, down, down . . .

I woke in a bath of sweat, my heart pounding, my shift plastered against me, but chilled from the nightmare. Day's first light shone through the one window in Peg's and my stuffy attic room. A wobbly wood table holding a pitcher of water separated our cots. A cracked white basin stood on the washstand against the back wall along with a small chest of drawers. Peg sat on the edge of her cot, coughing and coughing.

I hopped out of bed and poured her a glass of water. When she caught her breath, she sipped from the glass. "Thank ye, Katie," she murmured, pushing damp hair from her face. She sighed. "'Tis time for me to fire up the coals. 'Tis Mrs Reilly's washday."

"You stay in bed and catch your strength," I said, splashing my face with water. I rubbed my eyes with a rough cloth to clear the nightmare from my mind. But the worries wouldn't go away. If only Michael and Da didn't have to face Spike Wood and Weasel-face down on the docks every day. I shuddered, remembering Weasel-face's hate-filled eyes. And Miss Pratt – would she get me dismissed?

Peg's cough took hold of her again. When it ceased, she wiped her mouth with a cloth. Looking drawn and disappointed, she said, "Oh, but Michael's coming this morning to fill the coal bin."

"Michael will be awhile. I'll tend to the washtub coals. The coal dust always sets you coughing more."

Peg wiped her face with her hands. "Ah, Katie, thank ye kindly."

I combed and gathered my tangled hair into a coil and pinned it in place. "Maybe Michel will have news. Maybe there's been a letter from our mam."

Peg's smile lit her pale face. "'Twould be grand, Katie. I do hope your Patrick is on the mend."

"Faith, so do I. I wish Mam and Patrick were already here. 'Tis such a worry – that hard voyage ahead of them."

A look of longing veiled Peg's face. I knew she was thinking of the family she had lost.

"Now let me see," I said in Miss Pratt's clipped tones. I pulled open a drawer and pretended to search for something. "What hair-piece shall I add to my lovely curls today?"

Peg spluttered and laughed. "Ye sound just like the rat," she gasped. "Oh, that was a lark when Miss High and Mighty's hairpiece slipped and slid down her back."

I pinned my cap over my hasty hairdo. "And Elizabeth didn't help with her giggles."

I left Peg chuckling and skipped down the stairs. I heard Michael humming an unfamiliar tune before I saw him. I rounded the stairs and there he was – carrying a bucket of coal into the hallway between the kitchen and laundry. On the far side of the hall, a door opened into a coal bin. Michael's job was to fill it with buckets of coal from the outside bin.

"Morning to ye, Katie O'," he said, dumping black chunks into the bin. "And where's Peg? She's usually first one down on laundry day."

"Her cough's holding her back. She'll be down soon. Tell me, Michael, is there news from Mam? And is everything all right with you and Da? There's been no more trouble, has there?"

Michael leaned against the wall and drew his hand across his forehead, leaving a sooty smudge. "To answer your questions in order, Katie O', there's been no word from Mam and just the usual tension on the docks. Da tries to keep away from Big Spike. And in truth, I'm not down there much."

"Nothing yet, Michael?"

"Nothing. I'm tempted to work for Rooster, but Da's against it."

I nodded, secretly glad. Mr O'Donnell had been pelted with rubbish more than once now. And sometimes stones! "'Tis so confusing, Michael. I don't know who's right, Da or Mr O'Donnell and Mrs Reilly."

"Aye, Katie O', 'tis. But Rooster says the Irish have no power in Ireland, and if we want a say in what happens to us here, we have to elect a man who will help us. And 'tis only through voting we can to do that."

I frowned, still not sure, not wanting to go against Da.

"There's to be a rally at Faneuil Hall tonight for supporters of Richard Hunter. He's running for mayor. Rooster says he's not a member of the American Party but his views are the same. He says Know-Nothings are sure to be in be in the crowd whispering their secret passwords and giving their special handshakes. He says they'll be trying to recruit new members. And . . ." Michael stopped and bit his lower lip.

"And what . . . ?"

"Well, I'm worried Da might be there with that Dennis O'Malley."

"Will there be trouble, Michael?"

He shrugged and looked away. "Best we get on with our chores, Katie O'. I'll check the post later and if there's word from home, I'll bring it to ye in the park this afternoon. That is unless I find work." He picked up the bucket and started humming that unfamiliar tune.

"What's that you're singing, Michael?"

He stopped and made a face. "'Tis about us Irish. After all, if things are bad and ye can't change 'em?" he lifted a shoulder. "Why – we might as well sing about 'em, eh, Katie?" Holding the bucket to his chest and rolling his eyes upwards, he sang:

"I'm a decent boy just landed from the town of Ballyfad,
I want a situation, and I want it very bad.
I have seen employment advertised – 'Tis just the thing,'
    says I.
But the dirty spalpeen ended with 'No Irish need apply'.

Some do count it a misfortune to be christened Pat or Dan,
But to me it is an honor to be born an Irishman.

'Whoa,' says I, 'but that's an insult, though to get the
    place I'll try.'
So I went to see this blackguard with his 'No Irish need
    apply'."

"Oh, Michael, 'tis grand to hear ye singing first thing this
morning," Peg said, coming round the stairs.

"Thank ye kindly, Miss Pegeen," Michael said, lowering
the bucket and making a mock bow.

Peg blushed scarlet to the roots of her blond hair. I could
see she'd taken more care with fixing it this morning. She did
like Michael so.

Mrs Plumley called from the kitchen, "If you're through
with your concert, Michael O'Brien, you best get on with
your work. And you, Peg, get those coals started. Mrs Reilly
will be here and they'll be cold as death. And, Katie . . ."

"I'll do the coals, Mrs Plumley, then help in the kitchen."

Peg smiled shyly at Michael, then went upstairs to empty
the slop basins. Michael finished and left. But not before Mrs
Plumley had given him a good breakfast. She was always on
Peg and me to mind we didn't take extra, but she always fed
Michael when he did chores.

I set the coals to heating and was cleaning berries when
Mrs Reilly shot through the door. "Ach, 'tis hotter than
Hades out there this morning and no cooler in here," she
complained. She brought in the soapy smell that clung to
her. "Mornin' to you, Mrs Plumley, Katie."

"Mornin', Mrs Reilly." Mrs Plumley slid some muffins into
the oven, turned and folded her hands on her stomach. "Come
and have a sit down." She nodded her head at me. "Katie there
was a bit late with the coals this morning – talking with her
brother. You might as well have a cup of coffee and a bite of
blueberry bread." She sliced the day old bread.

"'Tis not good, Katie, being late," Mrs Reilly scolded. She pulled out a chair and sat at the table. "Thank you, Mrs Plumley. A rest and a bit of refreshment sounds just the right ticket."

Mrs Plumley poured two cups of coffee and heaved herself into a chair. "Tell me, Mrs Reilly, are you any closer to moving to Charlestown?"

Mrs Reilly nodded. "Aye, that I am. I should be there come early November."

"And ye'll be taking care of boarders?"

"And doing a bit of fancy ironing."

Mrs Plumley tapped her forefingers together and squinted at me. "Katie there did the ironing yesterday. I noticed a scorch smell here in the kitchen but I didn't hear any complaints from above stairs." Breathing heavily, she hoisted herself from her chair and pointed her chins toward the pantry. "Fetch me three eggs, Katie."

I set the berries to drain and reached for a towel. My neck muscles tightened. Mrs Plumley hadn't said a word about the smell. If Miss Pratt ever found that petticoat, I'd be in deep trouble. My mind in a whirl, I hurried to the pantry. I carefully chose three eggs and, making a pocket of my apron, turned toward the kitchen.

I recognized Miss Pratt's firm step on the stairs and a moment later she strode by the back entrance of the pantry. My heart raced. Whenever the rat came to the kitchen, it meant trouble. I stood in the front doorway of the pantry to listen. Her words set my stomach fluttering. "Mrs Plumley, Mr Pierce would like to see Katie O'Brien in his office immediately following breakfast."

I clasped my burning cheeks. The eggs fell and hit the floor with a splat. I stared at the gooey mess, then at the three women staring at me. Mrs Plumley's hands spread against her pillowy bosom. Mrs Reilly sat straight as a stick. Miss Pratt smirked. Her eyes narrowed and she looked straight at me. "Immediately after breakfast," she said precisely. She left the kitchen and the three of us, still as fence posts, listened to her stomp up the stairs.

12

Sacked

Mrs Plumley narrowed her eyes. "That woman!" She inhaled deeply and breathed out through her nose. "I hope her influence isn't too great with Mr Pierce, Katie." Shaking her head slowly, making her chins wobble, she said, "Clean up that mess now and bring me three more eggs. We've their breakfast to prepare."

Mrs Reilly, wringing her red hands, the knuckles as gnarled as tree knots, said, "Ach, Katie! What have ye been up to?"

"Nothing, Mrs Reilly," I stammered. No one knew Elizabeth had grabbed the iron and scorched her petticoat, did they? But then – there was the talk about lessons . . .

Mrs Reilly's gaze was steady and I felt my color rise. "There must be something."

"Well – Miss Pratt thinks I asked Elizabeth for lessons and . . ."

"Miss Elizabeth. Miss. Katie, ye must mind yer place. Lessons! Glory be. Aw, what's yer da to do? Michael with little to no work and in truth, 'tis likely ye'll be joining him." Her long nose quivered. "I must be off. I pray to the Holy Mother that ye don't get sacked."

It seemed like breakfast would never end. But when Thomas

came to take me to Mr Pierce, the time seemed to have whizzed by. I followed Thomas's rigid back up the stairs past the heavily draped, high-ceilinged entrance hall with the grand main staircase. Peg passed me carrying a covered chamber pot, a worried frown on her pale face. My throat tightened. I didn't want to leave Pierce House.

On the next floor, Thomas opened the heavy panelled doors that led from the servants' staircase and stepped into the hallway. Keeping his eyes straight ahead, he waited for me to follow, then closed the doors behind us. The latch clicked, cutting me off from the servants' quarters. Thomas turned toward the office at the front of the house.

"Katie," a light voice called. Elizabeth, looking flushed to the point of fever, tears brimming in her eyes, stood in the doorway of the music room. Before she could say another word, Miss Pratt appeared beside her, clamped a hand on the girl's shoulder and whisked her away.

Thomas opened the heavy office door and said, "Katie O'Brien, Mr Pierce, sir." Thomas beckoned me into the dim room. Deep red velvet drapes with gold tassels blocked the light from the bay window. Wood so dark it looked black framed the fireplace and added to the gloom.

Thomas glided from the room and shut the door firmly behind him. Squeezing my hands by my sides to keep them from shaking, I faced the man sitting behind the big desk. Flickering gaslight threw wavering shadows across his face.

For some time, Mr Pierce read papers and wrote. His skin puffed out like bread dough above his stiff white collar and neatly tied ascot. I stood there so long my knees began to tremble. Finally, he looked up. "Katie O'Brien, you've been here nearly a month now. Is that right?"

"Yes, sir."

"Yes. Mrs Plumley recommended you. And I agreed to a

month's trial over the objections of Miss Pratt." He said nothing for a moment, then, "Have we been unfair to you? Have you not a bed to sleep in, food to eat?"

"No, sir. Yes, sir," I mumbled.

"Then what is this Miss Pratt tells me about your wanting my daughter to teach you her lessons? Wanting her to educate you so that you may procure a better position?"

"It wasn't like that, sir. Elizabeth . . ."

"*Miss* Elizabeth," Mr Pierce corrected.

"Miss Elizabeth. She's very generous, sir. She wanted to share her lessons with us."

"And you didn't say that you wanted to leave my household, that you wanted to find better employment?"

Anger boiled up in me. "Faith, sir," I blurted. "Sure I don't want to be a hired girl all my life."

Mr Pierce stood. With pudgy fingers, he picked up a pen and slapping it against his palm, gazed at me. He wasn't nearly so tall as Da, but he had wide shoulders and a great head of dark hair, a little mustache and pointed cheek whiskers. Squinting, he asked, "Oh? And what is it you want to be?"

My head swung up and my chin jutted out. "I want to be a teacher."

"Um," Mr Pierce murmured. He sat again. "You may be a teacher one day, Katie O'Brien, but you'll learn your lessons on your own time. You are dismissed." He sat down in his chair, picked up his pen and bent his head to his papers.

I didn't move. Dismissed! Dismissed from the room? From the house?

I stood there a full minute or more.

Mr Pierce looked up. "Please, leave."

"Sir . . . you mean I am dismissed from the room?"

"You are dismissed from my employment. Take your things and leave today."

13

Tidings

I raced through the paths of the park to the bench where Michael and I met. Mr Pierce's words had settled in my middle and weighed me down. Peg had cried as I tied my few things – a change of drawers, my comb and my night shift – into a bundle. Mrs Plumley and even Thomas had been sorry to see me go. But worst of all, I'd not been able to say good-bye to Elizabeth. The thought of Miss Pratt filling Elizabeth's mind with hate for me made my throat swell with tears. And, then, to tell Michael and Da!

As I rounded a rhododendron bush, I saw Michael. He stood watching the men baling hay, a dejected droop to his shoulders. I was so glad to see him there. But then – that meant he'd found no work today.

"Michael!" My voice was thick with unshed tears. He didn't hear me. I cleared my throat and brushed at my eyes. I pushed my bundle deeper into one pocket and felt for the comfortable bulk of my books, *Robinson Crusoe*, *The Adventures of Ulysses* and *Grimms' Popular Stories* that Mr O'Donnell had bought me, in the other. I couldn't tell Michael I'd been sacked just yet. "Michael," I called again.

"There ye are, Katie." He nodded toward the working men. "I could help with the haying, eh? If they'd only hire me."

I watched the men wrap the cut hay and stack it in piles. They looked liked giant loaves of golden bread. A hot breeze carried the fresh-cut sweetness and bits of hay through the heavy air. An image of home flashed in my mind. "That you could," I said. "You always liked the haying."

Michael sighed. "The only part you liked was when we rushed down to the lough to cool off."

"The water was so cold it made my feet ache." I wriggled my swollen, throbbing feet. "In truth, it would be grand to dip them in the lough right now." With a piercing longing I wished I were home. Home with Mam and Patrick.

"Let's wade in the Frog Pond for a cool-off. 'Tis sure the heat in Ireland's nothing like this."

I tried to let my worries fall away as we walked to the pond. Michael yanked off his worn black boots and rolled up his trousers. I tugged off my too-tight boots and heavy cotton stockings and, holding up my skirt, splashed in after him. The cool water eased the fire in my feet. Michael flicked water in my face. Without thinking, I dropped my skirt and splashed him.

The wet cloth clung to my legs. "Look what you've made me do!" All the tenseness of the morning bubbled up and I burst into tears.

Michael hugged me, then led me from the pond to a bench. He kept his arm about me till my sobs quieted. "What is it, Katie O'? Have ye been sacked then?"

I nodded. "How did you know?"

The corners of his mouth turned up. "I know ye well, Katie. And I'm not surprised."

"Why, what do ye mean, Michael? I did all my chores and then some. And never a complaint."

"Aye. I know yer not one to shirk. But from what ye tell me, that Miss Pratt wanted ye out. Part of it being yer Irish. Part of it being the proud way ye have about ye. I'd guess 'tis from all the reading and talking ye did with Granny Shea. Sets ye apart, it does."

We sat silent for a few minuets, me wondering if what Michael said was true. "Ah, Michael, I've got to find another position."

"Ye will, Katie O'." He smiled , then took a deep breath and sang "Molly Malone", putting in my name as always. When he sang the chorus, he opened his eyes wide and made his brows dance. I tried to smile, but my mouth trembled. Michael's voice grew lower and softer,

"A – live, a – live o! A – live alive – o!
Crying 'Cockles and mussels, a – live, a – live o!'"

I rubbed my bare toes back and forth across the prickly grass, letting his singing calm me.

Michael sat back and pressed his hands against his eyes. "Ohhh, Katie, I can't find steady work. 'Tis time to work for Rooster or take my chance out west."

"No, Michael. Sure you'll find something." Then I remembered his talk of a political rally. I looked at him sideways. "Are you planning on going to that meeting tonight?"

Michael pulled a leaf from an overhanging branch and smoothed it against his palm. "Ye shouldn't be worrying yerself about politics. 'Tis a man's business."

"In truth, Michael, you're sounding like Da now. Mrs Reilly says that one day women will have the right to vote and she'll be the first in line."

Michael stood and grinned. "Faith, Katie, if that day ever comes, I'm thinkin' ye'll be right behind her. Now don't be getting' mad at me – that I waited to tell ye, but I've some good news this day. There's word from home."

I jumped up from the bench. "What? There's a letter and you're just telling me now?"

"Hold yer temper, Katie O'. I had my reasons. I could see ye were bursting with worry. Ye needed time to calm down a bit."

"Where is it? Where's the letter?"

Michael pulled a wrinkled envelope from his pocket and handed it to me.

"It's addressed to Da."

"Ye know Da doesn't read. Ye'll be the one to read it to him later."

I sat down and unfolded the paper. I touched the words Mam had written. I could see her sitting at the smalltable in our hut, crowding her words together to make the best use of the precious paper. At last, word from home. I read:

'My dearest Seán,

Thanks be to God our Patrick seems to be on the mend. No longer does he rave with fever. He is still weak but we pray every night that he will gain strength for our long journey to America. We will come soon as we can. We wait for news of you and the necessary fare for passage. Father Shaugnessy says to send your News and Earnings to us in care of Father O'Neill at St James's Church, Cork.'

My stomach lurched. I looked at Michael. "Why not to Father Shaughnessy?"

Michael scowled. "There must be new trouble. Read on, Katie."

My voice fading, I read:

'We have been warned that we must soon leave our land. All

village tenants will be evicted. If we don't leave our cottages will be torched, the Overseer tells us Lord M . . . needs the land for grazing grounds for his cattle. Joseph and Lily will travel to Galway to be with her family. There is no hope for the Irish in Ireland.'

I swallowed hard. Last year cottages in the next village had been torched. I shuddered, remembering the flames in the distance and the smoke-filled wind. My voice trembling, I finished the letter:

'Patrick sends love to you and his brother and sister as do I. We await the day our family will be together again, Keep heart and pray to the good Lord that Patrick will grow stronger each day.

From your loving wife till death
Nora O'Brien

Michael put his arm about my shoulders. Pulling me close, he said, "At least our Patrick is better."

I cried against his shoulder then wiped my face with my damp skirt. "Aye, but he's still weak, Michael. And to have no home! Where do you think they are now?"

"Probably Cork, staying in a room with the help of the church till they have the means to come here." Michael stood and toed the earth.

I clutched my hands into fists. "And now I've no work. Just when Mam and Patrick . . ."

He dug a newspaper clipping from his pocket. "Read this, Katie. Mr O'Donnell read it to me."

I took the grimy piece and read the caption: *Railroading the West – The Way to Success: Join the Union Pacific Railroad.* The article went on to promise good wages, fine food, excellent lodgings and steady employment.

No! No! No! roared in my head. Clutching the Holy Family medal, I read the article through more slowly. When I finished, I grasped Michael's arm and pleaded, "Don't go, Michael! Don't go! It's too far. I'll never see you again!" Suddenly angry, I shouted, "You want to go, don't you? You want to go out west and find that land you've always dreamed of."

Michael shook his head. "Ach, Katie, that's not fair."

My anger left as fast as it had come. "I'm sorry," I murmured. "But I don't want you to go. Mrs Plumley told us about her nephew. He went to work on the rails and no one's heard from him since."

Dragging both hands through his mop of red hair, Michael cried, "But we need money, Katie! Lest Mam and Patrick never get over." He paced back and forth over the dry grass. "And when they do come, 'twould be grand if we could move to Charlestown, like Mrs Reilly. The tenement's just wicked. The slops – people throw them into the streets. Sickness. Noise. No privacy. 'Tis no place to live!"

A frog croaked loudly. I looked up just as it splashed into the pond. The ripples spread on and out till they disappeared. Just like my family, I thought.

Michael stopped his pacing and knelt in front of me. He wiped a tear from my face. "Ah, Katie O', don't be looking so sad. I tell ye what. I'll give it another week. Then – it'll be Rooster or the rails."

I smiled. Another week. Anything could happen in a week!

14

The Meeting

Michael and I stuffed our feet into our boots. We walked along the park paths, crushing fallen rhododendron blossoms. The hot air, moist as a sopping dish-rag, pressed against me. I brushed a hand across my face, wiping away tear stains and sweat.

Michael picked a withered rose from a bush. Twirling it between his fingers, he sang softly:

> 'Tis the last rose of summer
> Left blooming alone;
> All her lovely companions
> Are faded and gone;
> No flower of her kindred,
> No rosebud is nigh,
> To reflect back her blushes,
> Or give sigh for sigh.

I knew he was thinking of Mam for it was her favourite song. No matter what happened Michael would sing. It was as much a part of him as breathing.

Outside Faneuil Hall, we dodged round horse-drawn

carriages piled high with produce. We entered the bustling Quincy Market, where the briny smell of fish mingled with the flavours of ripe fruit and vegetables. I wanted to make a nice tea for Da and thought I'd spend a bit of my last wages on a piece of fish and some vegetables. The rest would go to Da for Mam and Patrick's passage.

I was choosing carrots when a buzz of excitement went through the crowd. A tall well-dressed man, followed by other important looking-men, had entered. "That's Richard Hunter," Michael hissed.

A few people called out to him. He held up a hand in greeting, like a king. I shifted and angled myself to get a better look at him and caught the blaze of pale eyes in a long, sallow face. "He looks like he'd fight hard for what he wants," I said to Michael.

"Aye, he's not a rough-neck like Big Spike and Weasel-face, but Rooster says he's more dangerous. He says Hunter wants to pass laws to make it harder for us to become citizens and get the right to vote."

I watched Richard Hunter and his followers disappear up the stairs to the meeting room. "I wonder why they're here so early?"

"Probably making sure things are set for tonight."

Feeling uneasy, I chose a piece of codfish and some vegetables. Outside the market, Michael said, "Katie, you go on home and start tea. 'Tis nearing closing time for the stores. I'll try to earn a few pennies sweeping up."

An hour later, I had the vegetables simmering and the cod salted. I'd poach it in some vegetable broth after Da got home. I set bowls and mugs on the scarred table, then went to fetch more water for the tea. I hoped Michael would be here before Da. I dreaded telling Da I'd been sacked.

As I swung the kettle onto the stove, the door opened. I turned to find Da staring at me, eyes wide. "What are you doing here? What 'ave ye done?"

His words landed like blows. "Why nothing, Da," I cried.

He came in, bringing the oily smell from the docks with him. He whipped out a chair and sat down to pull off his heavy boots. Never looking at me, he said, "Ye've been sacked, haven't ye? I knew ye wouldn't last long."

Anger covered my hurt. "Why do you say that, Da? I worked hard, I did."

His bushy brows drew together. "Yer uppity, is why. Look how ye talk back to me. Think yer high and mighty, ye do!"

I turned and spooned boiling broth into a fry pan so fast it spattered my hands. But the burn didn't hurt as much as Da's words. I swallowed hard. I wouldn't cry – not in front of Da.

Da hoisted his right foot onto his left knee and massaged it. Must still be bothering him.

"What's this?" he asked, reaching for Mam's letter that I'd left on the table.

"Mam's letter. Michael brought it to me. He said you'd not mind if we opened it since . . ."

Brusquely, Da said, "Since ye'd have to read it to me anyway? Well, go on. Read it. What does yer mother write? 'Tis good news, I hope. I'm in need of some."

I sat at the table. With shaking hands and trembling voice, I read Mam's letter. When I finished, I glanced up to find him staring off into space. He murmured, "'Tis good Patrick's on the mend. But now – evicted." He turned to me and scowled. "Would have been better had ye stayed with yer Mam. Ye might have been some help to *her*."

My chin lifted and I stared right back at him. All the hurt and anger I'd felt since I'd come sprang from me. "You never did want me here, did you, Da? You never did want me at all. Why, you never even told Mrs Reilly about me!"

Da's hand swung out. "Watch yer tongue, Katie O'Brien. Yer not too big for a thrashing." He dropped his arm and nodded at the stove. "Serve up the tea. I've business to attend to tonight."

Da's only other words to me were to fill his bowl a second time. Michael didn't come in for tea. Had he got work cleaning out shops? Or . . . was he going to that meeting? What if he ran into Weasel-face? My stomach churned so I could hardly eat.

Da finished his tea, put his boots on and left. I wondered if he was going to join Dennis O'Malley. I covered the left-over food and hoped Michael would be home to eat it before it spoiled in the heat. I sat and stared at the dingy walls. I pulled *The Adventures of Ulysses* from my pocket but just stared at it, too jittery to read. I tucked it back into my pocket and left the tenement.

Outside, dusk was gathering in the narrow streets. My nerves felt tight as guitar strings as I half walked, half ran to Faneuil Hall. At the hall red letters on a blue banner bordered with white stars read:

VOTE FOR RICHARD HUNTER
PROTECT OUR NATION
FROM THE EVER-INCREASING
MULTITUDES OF FOREIGNERS.

The market stalls were covered and closed for the night. My heart thumping wildly, hoping no one would notice me, I climbed the stairs to the meeting room. Its heavy smell of heated bodies, beer and other spirits caught in my throat. I hid behind a post, looking in vain for a woman in the crowd. But it was all men, hardened workers, merchants, high-class looking gentlemen. And there was Michael – on the far side of the room. But no sign of Da.

Richard Hunter stood in front of the room, speaking. " . . . therefore, we need to protect our country from the cunning wiles of foreigners. We need to change our immigration policy. Far too many Irish are flooding our shores. Their attempted inroads into our political system threaten the stability of our proud Boston . . ."

He's using words, powerful words, to get what he wants, I thought. Just like Mr O'Donnell says. Richard Hunter doesn't want the Irish to vote. He's afraid of us. Mr O'Donnell, Rooster, and Mrs Reilly are right. Da is wrong!

I glanced over at Michael, easy to find with his height and red hair. My stomach dropped. Not far behind him was Patch-eye. I searched for Weasel-face.

"Well, look who's here." Weasel-face's voice, soft and menacing, shot through me like a bolt of lightning. He leered at me, so close I could feel the warmth of his stinking breath on my face. My mouth went dry. A strange light flickered in his eyes. The fear that had struck me on the wharf that day sang through every nerve.

He leaned closer. "Don't you know it's dangerous for little girls to be out at night?"

I shoved past him, elbowed my way through the crowd, bumped into a fat man.

He shouted, "Watch where you're going, girly."

A buzz went through the room.

"What's a girl doing here?"

"Looks pretty young to me."

I pushed on and darted down the stairs.

Weasel-face pounded down right behind me.

15

The Attack

I raced down the stairs. Outside, I sprinted past the north market, down to the waterfront. Weasel-face's footsteps echoed behind me.

Panicked, I ran blindly, past shacks, saloons and dark shops. The hot night air reeked of uncollected rubbish. The image of Weasel-face's eyes drove me on till I thought my chest would burst for want of air. A stitch in my side slowed me and I found myself in a busy section of the wharf. Rough voices and the squeal of girlish laughter came from grog shops. Sailors walked by with girls hanging on their arms. Two sailors whistled at me and called, "Hey, honey, want some company?"

I ducked my head low and hurried on. Had I lost Weasel-face? I darted a look over my shoulder. No sign of him. The fear racing through me quieted a little. I tried to place where I was. Past Rooster's Grog Shop. The tall masts of ships rose like skeletons above the black water. A buoy bell clanged low and mournful. If I could only turn around and walk straight back, I'd have no trouble finding my way home. But I didn't dare. Weasel-face might still be out there.

I hugged the buildings, avoiding the light of the dockside lamps. I'd have to take a chance on one of the alleys running between the warehouses and supply shops. One might lead me to a street I recognized, then I could find my way. I hurried by a fish shop, holding my breath against its oily stench. I walked on a little way – afraid to turn back, afraid to enter an unknown alley.

A group of loud, drunk sailors banged out of a saloon. One of them lurched towards me. "Hey, look what we've got here. Hey, doll, ya lost? Come to Ernie. Ernie will take care of ya."

The others laughed. One shouted, "Watch out for Ernie, sweetie!"

My temples pounded. I scooted into an alley, splashed through a puddle. Two sailors followed, bumping and banging into rubbish cans. One cried, "Look at the size of that rat! Come on, Ernie, let's get out of here. There's plenty girls down the way."

They left. I crept out from behind a rubbish barrel, my soggy hem clinging to my legs. I squinted into the alley. Oh, no – a blind alley! I stood there, hating to go back but knowing I'd have to. A rat, big as a cat, leapt from a rubbish can and whizzed by me. I stifled a scream and sped toward the wharf.

A shadowy form at the alley's mouth blocked my way. Weasel-face snickered. "So, this is where ya got yourself to?" He stole closer. "Trapped ya are. Alone – in a dark alley – just waiting for me."

My heart hammered against my ribs. I stepped back. Hesitated. At the end of the alley, I'd be further from help.

He stopped. In the shadowy light, I saw him wipe his hand across his mouth.

I'd wait for him to get closer. Then, I'd dart round him – back to the waterfront – back to people.

He took another step, like a cat ready to pounce. "Your big brother's not here to take care of ya now, is he, Katie O'Brien?"

I gasped. He knew my name.

"Oh, I know who ya are, all right. You and your brother and that big mouth O'Donnell. And I know you're Seán O'Brien's kid, the one gives Big Spike so much trouble."

He pulled something from his pocket. Moonlight glinted on steel.

He leapt toward me.

I bounded past him.

He seized my braids. A sharp pain tore through my head.

I screamed.

He yanked harder. Then his hand covered my mouth and he slammed my head against the building.

His hand – cruel – strong – crushing. My teeth cut into my lips. I struggled for air.

Bite him! Bite him! But I couldn't move my mouth. I spread my hands against his chest and pushed.

"Be still," he snarled, "or there's no telling what this knife will do." His hand twisted against my mouth and pressed ever harder.

His hand gone.

A gulp of air.

Braids yanked. My head wrenched back. Scalp puckering and tearing.

I felt removed, as though I'd left my body. I floated high above the alley. Moonglow sharpened everything – the rubbish, the barrels, a pile of wood. Smells strangled me – Weasel-face's sour breath, his stinking odour, the oily water.

His low evil voice. "Such a pretty little face. Just like a flower. Now how would that little face look with a slash? Say here?" He edged the knife along one cheek, not enough to cut, but I felt its sharpness. "And here." He edged the knife across my other cheek." His words turned into a crazy, high-pitched laugh.

The knife above me, glimmering in moonlight.

The knife slashing down, hacking off my braids. My head sprung forward. I floated back to my body.

Weasel-face reached for me again.

I kicked. My boot smacked against his shin.

He groaned and grabbed my arm.

I kicked and screamed.

Michael, with Patch-eye close behind him, flew into the alley. Michael pulled Weasel-face away from me, knocked him to the ground and, fists flying, fell onto him. Patch-eye picked up a jagged board, lifted it high and aimed for Michael's head.

"Michael!" I shouted.

Michael rolled off Weasel-face.

Patch-eye's weapon slammed down – cracked Weasel-face's forehead.

Weasel-face lay there, his forehead open and oozing – not moving, not making a sound.

The three of us froze. Then Patch-eye raised the gory wood and screeched at Michael. "You've killed him, you bloody Mick. You've killed him!"

16

The Back Room

Michael snatched my hand and we raced from the alley, down the waterfront, past warehouses and the great hulking ships. He pulled me into the shadow of a building as we neared a group of rowdy men.

He dropped his face into his hands and gasped for breath. I knew he was trying not to cry.

I put my shaking hands on his shoulders and squeezed hard. "Michael, you didn't kill Weasel-face. It was Patch-eye."

Michael wiped his hand across his eyes and nose and sniffed loudly. "Ach, Katie, who will believe a Mick?"

"But, Michael . . ."

"*Shh.*" He pushed me further into the shadows.

Patch-eye panted by shouting, "*Watchman! Watchman!* Murder!"

Michael shuddered and pulled me into another alley. This led to a back street that we followed till he turned down a narrow way, then turned again. We were in a byway that ran along the back of buildings. Rubbish cans overflowed. A large cat hissed at us and stalked away. Michel rapped on a door.

"Who's there?" someone called from inside.

"'Tis Michael O'Brien." His voice shook.

A skinny, bearded man opened the door a crack. I clutched my torn dress together. Michael pushed me through the opening, then followed. A gas lamp hung from a rafter, casting shadows in the storage room. The man motioned us to sit on some crates and left. He returned a minute later with two small glasses of amber liquid and handed one to each of us. Michael drank his in one gulp, coughed, then wiped his hand across his mouth.

"Take a sip, Katie O'," he said softly. "'Twill help settle ye."

I tried to sip the whiskey, but my hand shook so the glass clattered against my teeth. Suddenly icy cold, I was shaking uncontrollably. Great sobs burst from me and I cried and cried. Michael crouched by me and took me in his arms. He stroked the back of my head. I felt his hand stop and his fingers probe for my plaits. His voice quivered. "Ah, Katie, what he might of done to ye."

Rooster barrelled in with Mr O'Donnell right behind him. Mr O'Donnell's eyes and bristly beard threw sparks in the shadowy light. He made me choke down a sip of the whiskey. Its heat flowed to my stomach where it burst into a ball of fire. Then Mr O'Donnell wrapped me in a blanket and settled me among some sacks. He draped another blanket around Michael's shoulders and poured him another whiskey.

I shrank back into the sacks. Their rough warmth and the whiskey, hot in my centre, started to thaw my frozen body. A tinny piano tinkled in the tavern. My breathing slowed and I grew drowsy. I fought to keep my eyes open as Michael and the two men talked. Their voices droned on. Michael said over and over, "I tell ye. I didn't kill him. 'Twas Patch-eye."

"We don't doubt your word, Michael," Mr O'Donnell said.

"But 'tis best you get out of town," Rooster said, scratching the bald spot on his head. His words woke me up and I sat forward, every part of me listening.

"They'd arrest you and put you in jail as soon as they'd lay eyes on you. You know that, don't you, lad?" Mr O'Donnell said.

Michael, sounding more like himself, said, "Aye, 'tis so. They lock up an Irish for looking cross-eyed."

Chills ran up and down my spine. I thought of the frog I'd seen splashing into the pond today – how the ripples had spread out till they disappeared. I pressed my fingers against the Holy Family medal, then untangled myself from the blanket. Wobbling a little, I went and stood by Michael. "'Tis my fault, Michael. I should have stayed at Da's."

"No, Katie," Michael said. "Things would have come to a head sooner or later. Weasel-face has been out to cause me trouble since the day we got here."

"Where will you go, Michael?" I asked.

He looked from me to Mr O'Donnell then back. "'Tis time to hit the rails, Katie."

I traced the outline of the Holy Family with my fingers. An image of Mam, real and close, flashed in my mind. I thought of her promise. I slipped the medal over my head and held it out to Michael. "You wear it, Michael, till we're all together again."

Michael touched the medal with one finger. "No, Katie O', Mam gave it to you."

"Please, Michael," I begged, "then I know you'll come back."

He looked at me, then took the medal. Fumbling, he

unclasped the chain, then clasped it round his neck. He wiped a tear from my face. "I'll be back one day, Katie. I promise."

Rooster and Mr O'Donnell made the plans. Mr O'Donnell would go with me to the tenement. I would pack up Michael's few things and send them back with him. Then Donal, the skinny man who'd let us in, would take Michael to someone who would get him on the rails.

Mr O'Donnell brought me a jacket from one of the fancy ladies in the saloon, then we left by the back entrance. On the waterfront, we hugged the shadows. The night had an unreal quality. Sailors, dockers, men from the saloons with their fancy-dressed ladies hurried towards Faneuil Hall. Shouts sounded in the dark.

"Fight! Big fight!"

"There's been a murder!"

"A Mick did it."

The roar of many voices and breaking glass reached us. A watchman, shaking his rattle, raced by.

What was going on? Was it Dennis O'Malley's group and the Know-Nothings? Where was Da?

"It sounds as though the crowd has turned into a mob," Mr O'Donnell said. "I hope there won't be another fire. There's been a rash of them lately."

We walked up the narrow ways to Hull Street. Questions bumped about in my head. "Mr O'Donnell, why did Michael go to Rooster's? How did he know about that back door?"

"Ah, Katie. Michael has been searching his mind. He has been attending some of our meetings. He needed to determine for himself what he believes is the right thing to do."

"He told me he was thinking about working for Rooster, going against our da."

"Yes, he was."

"But it's dangerous."

Mr O'Donnell didn't say anything for a while, then, "There is some danger involved when men like Franky Wood, whom you call Weasel-face, and his like turn to violence. But if we don't work for what we believe in, Katie, there is more danger in that . . . You, yourself, put yourself in danger tonight. What were you thinking, going out on your own?"

I swallowed hard. 'Twas because of me Michael would be thought a murderer. "I know I should have stayed at Da's, Mr O'Donnell, but . . . I wanted to see what was going on. I wanted to know where Michael and Da were and I wanted to hear what that Richard Hunter had to say, and . . ."

"And what, Katie?"

"Well, I learned that you and Rooster are right and – my da is wrong."

"And that is what Michael has learned. If he had gone to work for Rooster, your father would probably have blamed me. He has no tolerance for my ideas. But fate has played its hand and soon Michael will be on his way west."

"Aye. 'Tis what he wanted."

"But not under these circumstances." Mr O'Donnell stopped and took me by the shoulders. "Michael will come back, Katie."

I nodded, wishing I could believe his words.

At the tenement, Da pulled the door open before I reached it. "Where have ye been?" He looked from me to Mr O'Donnell. "What's he doing here?" Then back to me. His eyes wide, he cried, "Holy Mother of God, what happened to ye?"

My knees suddenly weak and watery, I sank into one of

the wood chairs. I looked at Da. A small cut oozed blood on his forehead and a bruise darkened his cheek.

"Stop yer staring, Katie, and tell me what's happened to ye."

Faltering now and then, I told Da what had happened. I waited for him to explode but he sat still, his face stony. When I finished, he stood up without a word and gathered Michael's things. He gave them to Mr O'Donnell. His voice husky, he said, "Tell my boy I wish him God speed."

17

Scarlet Fever

Early next morning, I made oatmeal and tea for Da and me. Head bent, he ate silently, looking up at me every so often. When he finished, he frowned and his face hardened. "Best ye stay here today, Katie. Mrs Reilly's going to ask round for ye. God willing, she'll find ye something fast."

I nodded, not sure what Da was thinking. Was he blaming me for Michael's leaving? Last night, after Mr O'Donnell had left, Da had sat and stared at his hands. I had sat at the table, my hands clenched tight in my lap, trying to still the trembles starting through me again. After a time, Da had glanced at me, stood and muttered, "Best I get Mrs Reilly. Yer in need of a woman."

Mrs Reilly had come down and made us tea. She'd brought sugar from her own meagre supply. The strong, sweet tea had poured strength back in me and the trembling had stopped. Mrs Reilly hadn't said much for a change, but it was a comfort to have her there. After our tea, she'd cut my hair, trying to even it off. Now my head felt strange, lighter.

"Da . . . " My voice sounded hollow. "Da," I started again.

"I was thinking to check the hotels today, to see if they need a cleaning girl, then if Mrs Reilly doesn't . . ."

Da slapped his hand on the table, making the dishes jump. "Yer to stay here in this room till Mrs Reilly finds ye something. Jesus, Mary and Joseph! Don't ye realize yer in danger? Now I'm thinkin' on it best ye stay in Mrs Reilly's room. Once they find out where Michael lives, the police will be round."

Startled, I said, "But . . ."

"There ye go, being uppity again. No buts. You listen to yer da . . ."

A knock at the door stopped him. Scowling, he muttered, "Sure it can't be them yet." He glanced at me, then called, "Who's there?"

"Thomas Johnson, Mr Pierce's butler."

My heart lurched. What was Thomas doing here?

Da opened the door.

"Is there where Katie O'Brien lives?" Thomas asked in precise tones.

"'Tis," Da said cautiously.

"I've a message from Mr Pierce of Pierce House. His daughter, Miss Elizabeth, is down with fever. She keeps calling for Katie. Mr Pierce says Katie O'Brien is to come back to his service."

Thomas waited in the hackney coach Mr Pierce had sent him in while I gathered my things. Just before I left, Da said, "Ye've another chance. Don't bungle it."

As the driver threaded the coach through the streets, men trudging through the hot, muggy morning, stopped and stared at the unfamiliar sight. I shrank back against the seat, not wanting to be seen.

Thomas's expression hadn't changed when he saw me, but I knew he'd noticed my short hair. He sat ramrod straight beside me and would tell me only that, "Miss Elizabeth is sick with fever and is calling for you." I knew I'd have to wait till I got to Pierce House to find out how sick she was. The driver pulled the horse to a stop by the ally entrance. While Thomas paid him, I rushed down the ally to the brick courtyard.

I pushed open the shed door. Mrs Plumley, her face the colour of strawberries, glanced up from the block of ice she was chipping. "Lord's sake, I'm glad you're here, Katie. Miss Elizabeth's been calling for you and Mr Pierce is beside himself. Peg and me are worn to a frazzle, what with running up and down the stairs doing Miss Pratt's every little bidding."

"Is Elizabeth bad off?"

Her eyes widened. "Dear God almighty! What happened to your hair?"

My hand shook as I ran it over my curls. "'Tis nothing, Mrs Plumley," I said, not wanting to remember last night. "I'll hide it under my cap."

"You've circles deep as black holes under your eyes." A worried frown creased her forehead but she didn't press me for details. "Well, to work. Get on with chipping the ice. There's the jug for it." She handed me the ice pick and nodded toward a large blue jug set on a shelf. "Then fill it with water and take it on up to Miss Elizabeth's room." She collapsed on a stool that groaned beneath her weight. Shaking her head, chins wobbling, she went on. "Dr Hawkins is with the child now, though it's so early. She had a bad night of it." She rubbed an ice chip across her face. "Best you make yourself presentable, Katie. Then hurry up with that jug. Peg's just gone up with one."

I pulled an apron from a hook and tied it round my waist and jammed my short hair under a cap. I filled the jug with ice and water and started up the stairs to the fourth floor nursery.

On the third floor, I met Peg coming down with an empty jug. "How's Elizabeth?" I asked.

Peg pushed strands of hair back from her thin face. "'Tis bad she is, Katie. She . . ." A cough stopped her. Blood rushed to her face, colouring it pink, then red. Finally, the cough left her. Wiping tears from her eyes, she said hoarsely, "She calls out for you, she does. Send up a prayer for her, do."

I climbed the rest of the stairs and stood outside the closed door of Elizabeth's room at the back of the house. I could hear the murmur of voices. I placed the jug on the floor and knocked. The voices stopped. Miss Pratt, reeking of her heavy floral scent, opened the door. "Please, Miss Pratt, how is . . . ?"

"Empty this, Katie," she commanded, picking up a covered chamber pot stinking of vomit. "And be sure you clean it thoroughly."

A short, trim man, standing beside Elizabeth's bed, looked at me. "Is this the 'Katie' Elizabeth has been asking for?"

Miss Pratt turned, her full-skirted figure blocking me. "Yes, Dr Hawkins. But she's just a kitchen girl."

"Bring her in."

I picked up the water jug and stepped into the dim, sour-smelling room. Heavy rose drapes covered the bay window that faced the alley. Elizabeth's bed stood against the wall to the left. Double doors to the right led to Miss Pratt's room. I walked past Miss Pratt, who still held the foul chamber pot. She glared at me, set the pot by the door, then came to stand at the foot of the narrow bed.

A fiery flush coloured Elizabeth's cheeks. She whimpered and moved restlessly. A white blanket, soft as a cloud, covered her. Her brown curls, now a mass of snarls, spread over a lace trimmed pillow. The doctor took the jug from me and emptied the water into a china basin. He wet a towel, wrung it out, and placed it on Elizabeth's forehead. He smoothed the wet cloth with firm but gentle movements. Elizabeth sighed and quieted.

Dr Hawkins looked at me with kind gray eyes. "Do you think you could do what I'm doing now, Katie?"

I darted a look at Miss Pratt. Why wasn't she tending to Elizabeth? I wondered.

Dr Hawkins answered my unspoken question. "Elizabeth becomes more agitated when Miss Pratt touches her. She calls for you. Do you think you could keep cool cloths on her head?" he asked again.

I nodded. "Yes, sir, I did the same for my brother back home." An image rushed into my mind – Patrick, tossing on a thin mattress, covered with a worn blanket.

The doctor watched as I took the towel, already hot, from Elizabeth's forehead. I dipped it into the basin, wrung it out and smoothed it on her brow. "Katie," she murmured. In less than a minute, the cloth was hot again. I removed it, soaked it with cool water and replaced it.

The doctor nodded his approval. "I want you to keep the cloth wet and cool. Miss Pratt, would you fetch more linens, please?"

Miss Pratt scowled, then huffed out of the room. A moment later, she returned with a pile of towels.

"Now, Katie," the doctor said, taking the towels, "we must cool Miss Elizabeth down. You must keep wet cloths on her forehead and wrists and bathe her arms and legs." He lifted Elizabeth's lace-trimmed gown and placed wet towels on her knobby-kneed legs.

Suddenly, Elizabeth clutched her stomach and retched. I grabbed for the basin, but vomit gushed from her and soiled the bed.

I held the basin while the doctor turned Elizabeth's head

to the side. Now she just heaved and heaved but nothing came up. The door opened and Mr Pierce strode in. He looked at me and nodded slightly. Holding a white handkerchief to his nose, he came to the bed and gazed down at his daughter. "Elizabeth, can you hear me, my dear?"

Elizabeth tossed and moaned. Tears ran from beneath her eyelids.

"Miss Pratt, Katie, please clean Miss Elizabeth up." Dr Hawkins ordered, taking Mr Pierce by the elbow. The two men left the room and Miss Pratt and I stared at each other.

"Fetch clean sheets, girl," she snapped, pulling the soiled sheets loose from under the mattress. "And be quick about it."

I hurried to the linen closet in the hall. Dr Hawkins and Mr Pierce were talking in low tones at the far end. I strained to hear what they were saying, but could only make out a word or two. What did Elizabeth have? I wondered. Was it the same fever that had sickened Patrick? Please God, make little Elizabeth better like Patrick. I reached for my Holy Family medal. Gone! Michael leaving! And now Elizabeth . . .

Miss Pratt had tucked the soiled sheets under Elizabeth's feverish body. She took a clean one from me and spread it on her side of the bed. She pulled Elizabeth toward her with a quick, forceful movement. Elizabeth cried out. I scooped the dirty linens from the bed and pulled the clean sheet under Elizabeth while Miss Pratt pinned the little girl still.

I bit my tongue to hold back angry words. She doesn't like Elizabeth anymore than she likes me, I thought. With Elizabeth comfortably settled, I started bathing her again. The door cracked open and Mr Pierce peeked in. Immediately, Miss Pratt said in pleasant tones, "Katie, take those soiled linens down to be washed. I'll bathe Miss Elizabeth."

My eyes opened wide and I stared at her. Such a changeling! Suddenly her voice was soft and her manner gentle. Then I remembered Peg saying how Miss Pratt hoped to be the next Mrs Pierce.

I picked up the sopping linens. Mr Pierce still stood in the doorway, rubbing his fingers across his mustache. Why doesn't he come in? Surely, Elizabeth would welcome his voice and touch.

"Miss Pratt," he said, dropping his hand to his side. She looked over at him, an expectant smile on her face. "Miss Pratt and Katie, my daughter has scarlet fever. Dr Hawkins says that the two of you and Peg, who will be nursing Miss Elizabeth, should not leave the house. He hopes this will help to keep the disease from spreading."

Miss Pratt's smile left her face. Her eyes widened. "Not leave the house? What about a nurse? Doctor Hawkins said he would send a nurse."

"Yes, if he can find one. But there's a great deal of scarlet fever about and he's not certain a nurse will be available. He'll be back tomorrow to check on Elizabeth." He left, pulling the door shut behind him.

Miss Pratt turned furious. "Take those filthy linens down, then get back up here and bathe this child." She spun on her heel and, wide hips swaying, disappeared through the double doors.

A jumble of thoughts whirred through my head. Closed in. No more walks in the park. Michael leaving. Closed in with Miss Pratt!

Elizabeth groaned. I dropped the linens and went to her. I dipped a towel into the clean water remaining in the basin and bathed her forehead, arms and legs. The cloths heated quickly. I repeated the process. Elizabeth calmed. Her brown eyes opened. She seemed to recognise me and smiled.

A rap sounded on the door. "Yes?" I called.

The door opened and Peg came in with a full jar of water. "How is she?" she whispered.

I laid my hand on Elizabeth's forehead. Heat came right through the wet cloth. "She's burning."

Peg hurried over and poured fresh water into the china basin. I reached out and touched her arm. "You and me, Peg," I said, "we'll nurse her back to health."

Peg looked doubtful. She nodded. "Aye, Katie, we'll try."

I swallowed the panic rising in my throat. "We can do it, Peg. We can!"

"With God's help," she murmured.

I nodded and crossed myself. "With God's help."

18

Fever Strikes Again

"Katie, I can't hear you," Elizabeth grumbled. She raised her head from her pillow and thumped the mattress with her hand, releasing puffs of lavender-scented air.

"Ah, Elizabeth, 'tis just that I'm so tired," I mumbled, dropping *Tales of Mother Goose* into my lap. I reached over to rub flaky skin from her arm. A few weeks ago she'd been covered with a fiery rash. She'd looked like a boiled lobster. Then the rash turned to rough spots. Now patches of skin were peeling from all over her body, as though she'd had a terrible sunburn.

I leaned back in my chair and yawned. It was only midday and I longed to sleep. My eyes felt gritty and my throat sore. The words of the book kept blurring. "I can hardly keep awake, Elizabeth."

"How come?" Elizabeth asked.

I yawned again. "I slept poorly last night." In truth I'd hardly slept at all. A few weeks ago, Peg had found an old Battledores alphabet book in the trash. The letters and pictures on the heavy, folded cardboard were crumpled and spotted but still readable. Whenever we had the time and energy, I'd help her with her studies. Last night, after we'd finished, Peg had fallen right to sleep, but I'd tossed and turned, hot, then cold.

Miss Pratt flung open the double doors to her room and her heavy perfume drifted in like a dark cloud. She stood a moment, staring at us. Elizabeth pulled her covers up to her chin. I straightened in my chair and picked up the book. Miss Pratt lifted her head and glided to the bed. She'd changed from the dress she'd worn when we bathed Elizabeth earlier. Tortoiseshell combs shone in her tightly upswept hair. She bent and touched her fingertips to Elizabeth's forehead. Elizabeth shrank into the pillows.

Miss Pratt's face tightened. "Dr Hawkins is expected shortly. He and your dear father should be pleased. I'm sure you no longer have a fever. Sit up, dear. You're all in a rumple." She fluffed the pillows and folded the sheet neatly over the blanket. "What's this? You've spilled something on your shift." She made a disgusted sound with her tongue and teeth. "I'll get you a clean one."

Another huge yawn rose all the way from my feet. Miss Pratt slid her eyes to me. "Cover your mouth, Katie O'Brien," she snapped. "You've been granted a special privilege, sitting in here reading to Miss Elizabeth. You might keep your wits about you." She pointed to a silver tray on the bedside table holding the remains of a cup of beef-tea. "Take that down and bring up a fresh cup and a slice of toast with grape jelly for Miss Elizabeth." She swept to the bureau and started rummaging through the drawers.

I plodded downstairs to the kitchen, put the dirty dishes in the sink and placed a clean linen napkin on the tray. The kettle holding steaming beef-tea felt twice as heavy as usual. I poured the tea into a clean china cup, then toasted a slice of bread. The heat from the coal stove seemed to simmer in my body.

I lifted the tray and trudged up the stairs. With each step my legs grew heavier and the stairs grew higher. Outside Elizabeth's door, I heard Miss Pratt's voice raised in anger. I nudged the door with my foot and stood in the opening.

Through a haze, I saw Miss Pratt holding up the scorched petticoat that Elizabeth had hidden away so long ago. Elizabeth sat forward and clasped her hands to her chest. "Katie didn't do it. I did it. Don't tell my father. He might make Katie leave again!"

Miss Pratt's voice seemed to come from far away. "You did it? You? You were ironing?"

All the things I'd like to say to Pratt the *rat* whirred through my head, but nothing came from my mouth but the chattering of my teeth. Miss Pratt started to sway to and fro. She loomed large, than small. Her voice floated away, near. Waves of fire, then ice, surged through me. The tray fell from my hands and crashed to the floor. I reached for the door frame and collapsed.

Through a fog, I looked up at Mr Pierce and Dr Hawkins leaning over me. Mr Pierce jerked a handkerchief from his pocket, held it to his nose and disappeared from my view. Dr Hawkins crouched next to me. His hand felt cool on my forehead, his fingers gentle as he felt my throat. His gray eyes looked worried. "It looks like we have another one down with scarlet fever," he said. "Katie had best be put to bed."

I heard Mr Pierce's muffled voice. "Ring for Thomas, Miss Pratt."

Then Elizabeth, sounding wobbly, "Katie! Katie, are you all right?"

Then Dr Hawkins, "Miss Pratt, help Miss Elizabeth back to bed."

Then Thomas carried me up to my attic room and lay me on my cot. I drifted in and out of consciousness. Chills slashed through me. Weasel-face's evil eyes glinted above me.

Gentle hands undressed me, then slipped my shift over my head. Someone placed a cool cloth smelling of vinegar on my forehead, then removed it. "Faith, Mrs Plumley, she's hotter than Miss Elizabeth was at her worst."

I wanted to thank Peg for the cool cloths but my tongue wouldn't work and my throat felt swollen. I opened my eyes and tried to smile my thanks, but shut them fast for the light pained me.

Images haunted me: Huge hands tossing Maggie into the black sea, Mam and Patrick fleeing a fire that dogged their steps, Michael spinning further and further away, and always Weasel-face – leering, threatening.

19

Sisters

After the first week, Dr Hawkins said I'd passed the crisis and would now begin the long road to recovery. Each day I gained strength, the glands of my neck – swollen to twice their normal size – began to soften and grow smaller. My ears still ached, especially the right one, but Dr Hawkins said there was no sign of an abscess. On the tenth day, I crawled out of bed and washed myself at the basin. Peg, coming in with tea and toast cried, "Katie, ye should not be up yet."

"I'm well enough to tend myself and help a bit in the kitchen," I said, buttoning my dress. The room spun slightly and black spots danced before my eyes. I sat on the edge of the bed.

"There – ye see, you're weak as a kit . . ." She started coughing. When she caught her breath, she poured me a cup of tea.

I sipped the hot liquid gratefully, its warmth giving me strength. "Thank you, Peg. You've nursed me back to health. You're a true friend, ye are."

Peg kissed me lightly on the cheek. "Ach, Katie, yer like a sister to me, don't ye know!" She brushed tears from her eyes.

I stood and hugged her. "And you to me, Peg. I'll not have you up and down these stairs all the day long. I'm coming down to help in the kitchen."

The next day, Mrs Reilly came to do the wash. "Yer Da's been askin' after ye, Katie. Worried he is. And he would of come to see ye but the doctor said no visitors. He'll be right pleased to know yer on the mend."

Her words sent little bubbles of happiness through me. Da had asked how I was doing!

Gradually, the household began to recover its normal order. Though I tired easily, I'd taken up most of my chores by the week's end. Miss Pratt resumed Elizabeth's lessons and made sure Elizabeth didn't visit the kitchen. When Mrs Reilly came the next washday, I hoped for a post from Michael, but nothing. And every morning I leafed through the day-old paper that Thomas always saved, looking for news of Weasel-face's death and the search for Michael O'Brien. Again nothing. And Mrs Reilly had told me that the police had never shown up at Da's tenement.

About a week after I'd left my sick bed, I spread the paper on the table and searched it once again. Peg, flushed and thinner than ever, waited by me. She was the only one who knew what had really happened that terrible night. And every night, we prayed together to the Holy Mother to watch over Michael and guide him safely. I looked up from the paper and shook my head.

"Ah, Katie, sure 'tis good there's naught in the papers. And for sure Michael will get word to ye soon."

Mrs Plumley came in carrying a milk jug from the shed as

117

Peg started for the pantry to collect the breakfast eggs. Suddenly, Peg bent forward, clutching her middle and vomited.

Mrs Plumley rushed to her. "Dear, Lord, I've been worrying on this. Peg so frail and all. Run to Mr Pierce, Katie. Ask him if Thomas might be sent for Dr Hawkins again."

20

Howl of the Banshee

I spooned ice chips to Peg's cracked and bleeding lips. Her tongue, a huge strawberry, all red and pitted, darted out for the moisture, but Peg never opened her eyes. I dipped a cloth in the bowl of vinegar water and laid it across her forehead. She tossed and turned and the bran poultice round her throat fell away. Her swollen throat struggled to swallow the few drops of water. A cool October breeze blew through our one window but did little to freshen the attic room.

I looked at the jagged piece of slate with Peg's name printed on it that lay on the table between our beds. She'd rescued the slate and bits of chalk from the rubbish . She'd worked so hard to learn her letters. Now, for the past week, she'd just lain in bed, too weak with fever to do anything. "Open your eyes, Peg," I pleaded. "Soon as you're better, we'll start our lessons again."

The call bell jangled, coming from the music room, where Elizabeth practiced the piano with Miss Pratt. Every day she'd ring for iced juice at just this time. I'd tried to leave it earlier this morning so I could spend more time with Peg, but Miss Pratt wouldn't have it. She'd insisted I wait till she called for it. I'd bit my tongue, holding back angry words, Da's warning not to be uppity ringing in my ears.

I squeezed Peg's dry hand. Then I picked up the poultice, planning to bring a fresh one, and hurried down the stairs. I met Mrs Plumley, huffing up from the kitchen with the juice and a few cookies on the linen-covered silver tray. "Thank you, Mrs Plumley," I said, taking the tray from her.

Breathing hard, she tugged at her tight collar and took the poultice from me. "I'll fix a fresh one for Peg," she said. She looked at me and shook her head making her white cap bob. "You're wearing yourself out, Katie. You're looking pinched and pale and those circles under your eyes are dark as your hair. You be sure to take your rest time this afternoon or you'll be down sick again. I'll see to Peg. You need to take some good air in the park."

Worry fluttered in my stomach. "Mrs Plumley, Peg's not talking. Not a word! She doesn't seem to know I'm there."

Mrs Plumley's mouth tightened. "Dr Hawkins is due to check in on her today." She lumbered down the stairs.

I crossed myself and prayed that Peg would be all right, that soon she'd be like Elizabeth and me, better and better each day. But the worry wouldn't go away. The call bell jangled three times, loud and angry over the sound of a piano scale. I carried the silver tray to the music room.

Red, orange and yellow leaves swirled through the air and scurried along the ground. I liked crunching and crackling them under my feet as I walked along the park paths. This cold, dry air, so different from the bone-chilling damp of Ireland, was such a relief after the roasting summer days.

I fingered the pages of Michael's letter tucked into my skirt pocket. I couldn't wait to read it. Mrs Reilly had stopped by with it just as I was leaving. I'd ripped the envelope open and saw it was from Michael, then folded it back in my pocket. I would read it in the park. I hoped it was good news, not worrisome like Mrs Reilly had told me yesterday about Da. I hadn't seen Da in a while, not being able to leave the Pierce house till just this week. Dr Hawkins had finally said there was no need for Miss Pratt and me to stay cooped up in the house anymore. Thank the Lord!

Yesterday, when I was helping Mrs Reilly with the wash, she'd told me about Da. The laundry room smelled of hot water and lye. A cool draft of air came through the ground-level window set high in the wall. Mrs Reilly, her sharp elbows pumping up and down as she sudsed Mr Pierce's shirts, said, "That Spike Wood will be the death of yer da, Katie, sure as the leaves are changing color."

"What happened, Mrs Reilly? Tell me! Is Da hurt again?"

She shook her head and a drop of sweat flew from the tip of her nose. "He's all right, Katie. It'll take more than a few hard knocks to keep yer da down. Spike Wood never takes yer da on alone these days. Yer da's not as big as that bully, but he's mighty good with his fists. Beat Wood fair and square one day. Now Wood's always got his toughs with 'im."

She flung the shirt to me and I sloshed it in the rinse water. Her words sharp, she went on. "He's acting strange, yer da says. Never came right out and said Michael killed that no-good nephew of his. Course we know it was that Patch-eye. Seems he's the one talks about the murdering O'Briens and how they'll get theirs one day. 'Tis probably his guilty conscience, that is if the likes of him's got a conscience."

I wrung the shirt and kept myself from snapping at her. Would the woman ever tell me what happened? "Well then, Mrs Reilly, did they beat Da?"

"Shoved 'im around a little. Threatened 'im. Said they knew he was with O'Malley's United Irish and he'd better watch his step."

I wished I could talk to Da. Better yet, I wished Da would listen to Mr O'Donnell. Sure he'd come to see joining the United Irish wasn't the thing to do. A whirlwind of leaves scuttled across my path. I took a deep breath of the cold frosty air. I fingered the letter in my pocket. How I wished Michael were here. I missed him so!

When I reached the bench by the pond, I pulled his letter out. I drew my feet under me against the nip in the air and smoothed the pages on my lap. I pictured the Holy Family medal Mam had given me resting on Michael's chest. It made me feel nearer to him.

My dear Katie O',

America is a great country and the tracks I lay each day make it greater Ah, Katie the land so much land. Each day we lay at least a mile of track as we make our way into the Louisiana Purchase Territory – but the land goes on and on endless like – grass tall as a man far as the eye can see like when we sailed to America and saw naught but ocean – Sometimes we see a few trees by a tricklin' stream – not like our Lough and green hills back home – herds of great beasts they call buffalo roam the land. 'Tis a grand sight they are – but Tuesday last we saw a great many laying dead. Pat who hails from Dublin and writes these words for me told me hunters kill them off for sport and to make room for the cattle – the waste of it and All the Hunger back Home – 'tis a evil thing – Pat says the killin' of the great beasts will help rid the land of Indians – we send out patrols watchin' for Indians – Sometimes they attack railworkers – but so far we have no trouble with them – Pat and most of the Irish workin' here send their earnin's to family back in Ireland. Last week I sent my months wages to Mam – no empty letter from me – 'Tis a good feelin Katie to be helpin' Da send for Mam and our Patrick.

Some call the trains mechanical demons what with their spittin' fire and burning cinders. A whole city follows us, Katie – A supply train puffing streams of smoke, holding rails, ties and spikes comes from the nearest city to the end of the line – the noise of it – the clangs and shreeks of the Iron Monster scare the buffalo and they go galloping off sending up great clouds of dust Men load the supplies onto horse-drawn wagons that bring it to us – the Iron Men, ah, you would not believe how strong they are – Five of them stand on either side of the track and lift a rail wayin near 36 stone 500 pounds they call it here, and drop it in place – well Katie Sure I'm no Iron Man – I'm a Spiker, we hammer spikes through wooden ties that connect the rails – there's a rithum to it 'Tis like music and it runs through my head all day and all the night – 3 strokes to a spike ten spikes to a rail four hundred rails to a mile – There's Contests to make us work harder and faster - if a team lays more than a mile in a day we get extra tobacco and Double Pay.

'Tis not easy work Katie – but 'tis good to be workin – we have enough to eat – cattle they drive along next us and the great buffalo – we sleep in boxcars with no windows – the sides are lined with Bunks three on top of each other – 'Tis close, Katie – and brings to mind our time in steerage. The air smells bad and the bedbugs bite fierce and raise welts on my skin – 'tis better sleepin' outside – I make up a bed roll and sleep with my rifle right next to me – the stars look so close you could reach up and grab one.

But night thoughts get fearsome and keep me from sleep. I close my eyes and see Weasel-face – him attackin' ye – then him stretched out on the ground – still and bleedin'. Oh, Katie, that such a thing happened!

I try to wipe the picture away and turn my thoughts to the land – the good Lord willin' the day will come when Michael O'Brien will own a piece of it – Aye I'll not have to answer to any landlord

I'm missin' ye Katie O' – ye and Da. When ye read this to him tell him his son sends greetin's.

Your loving brother,
Michael

I pulled the small geography book Elizabeth had given me from my pocket. When I'd told her about Michael going out west, she'd loaned me the book of maps. "You keep this as long as you like, Katie," she'd said. "You can follow your brother's trip on the map."

I studied the states stretching across the land. Where was Michael? Iowa? The Great Plains of Nebraska Territory? So many miles between us! I rested my head back against the bench and looked up through thinning leaves. A few white clouds floated in the blue sky. The west sounded so different from this Boston I'd landed in and so far away. Would Michael come back? He dreamed of owning land as much as I dreamed of going to school. A great loneliness settled in me. Would I ever see Michael again?

My eyes grew heavy. I was tired, so tired. My right ear throbbed, a reminder of the fever. And now Peg. When I got back I'd go up to her, bathe her again. "Dear God," I prayed, "let her be better. Let her know me." I closed my eyes and drifted off. I dreamed of bathing Peg, dipping a cloth in the basin of water, wringing it out, placing it on her hot skin, all mixed up with images of racing buffalo, endless stretches of land and Michael hammering spikes.

A howl woke me. Terrified, I sat up so fast my head reeled. There it was again. Goosebumps rose on my skin and my heart rose in my throat. The sound pierced my ears. My eyes scanned the park. Outlined against the setting sun was a big black dog, head thrown back, howling like a banshee.

I jumped up from the bench and ran down the path, scattering dead and dying leaves.

21

Death

I raced through the park, not slowing till I reached the alley. Breathing hard, I started down the passage, dim and shadowy in the fading light. A black horse and wagon stood in the narrow way. The horse whinnied and shook its head. Why was a wagon there? Morning was the time vendors filled the alley with their carts brimming with produce and when Mrs Plumley, a determined look in her eye, went out to barter. This was the first time I'd seen a wagon there at this time of day.

My neck prickling, I walked closer. The wagon waited at the Pierce courtyard. The driver, a ragged old man, was lowering its hinged back.

The shed door opened and Thomas came out carrying a bundle wrapped in a white sheet. The image of another bundle hurdling down to black water flashed before me and shivers crept up my spine. Mrs Plumley walked close behind Thomas. The wind caught the shed door and slammed it back and forth. Thomas stopped mid-step when he saw me. His sombre face crumpled.

"No, Thomas! No!" I shouted, running to him and grabbing his arm.

Mrs Plumley pulled me to her. "Young Peg has died, Katie."

"She can't be dead. She can't!"

"She was gone when Dr Hawkins went up to her," Mrs Plumley said.

I clung to Thomas's arm, "No!" I cried. "No!"

Mrs Plumley put her arm round my shoulders. "Let Peg go with dignity, Katie."

"Dignity?" I screamed, letting go of Thomas and pulling away from Mrs Plumley. "Dignity! What dignity did Peg have? Her working so hard to learn her letters, wanting to be a shop girl. Dignity? Sure, they don't even take her out the door! The back door's good enough for the likes of us, even in death!" I covered my face with my hands and burst into tears.

Mrs Plumley squeezed my shoulders and pulled me against her. Making soothing sounds, she reached into her pocket and handed me a clean cloth. Thomas walked to the wagon and gently laid Peg on its bed. He stepped back and bowed his head. The driver lifted the back and latched it in place. He climbed into the driver's seat, lifted the reins and said, "Giddap". The horse, head hanging low, plodded down the alley. I pictured Peg's thin body pitching about in the wagon.

Thomas's eyes glistened. He touched my shoulder gently, then disappeared into the shed, leaving the door to bang to and fro in the wind. Mrs Plumley stood by me and we watched the wagon journey the length of the alley. Then it turned into the street and vanished from sight. I looked up at Mrs Plumley who was dabbing at her eyes with her apron. "Where are they taking her, Mrs Plumley?" I whispered.

"For a pauper's burial, child. As you know, Peg was an

orphan, no family at all." She blew her nose, then said, "Come along, Katie," and led me to the door.

I stepped into the kitchen. Warm air on my chilled skin made me shiver. I looked around as though in a dream. Everything looked the same, bread rising under a cloth on the stove, the chopping-block and knives on the centre table. But Peg was dead.

Mrs Plumley pulled bits of leaves from my hair. "You're all windblown." She laid her hand on my curls. "Your hair's growing in fast, Katie." She sighed, then shuffled to the stove, bent and poked at the coals. "'Tis time to prepare another meal," she muttered. Straightening up, her face all flushed with exertion, she said, "I can handle it alone tonight. You need some time to yourself. Go on upstairs."

My heart feeling like a lump of cold coal, I plucked my apron from a hook on the wall. "No, Mrs Plumley. I thank you, but I'll be doing my regular chores," I said, not wanting to go to the room I'd shared with Peg.

Light steps pattered down the stairs. Elizabeth rushed into the kitchen. She threw her arms about me and sobbed. "Oh, Katie, I saw from the window. Miss Pratt wouldn't tell me what the wagon was for but I begged Thomas and he just told me. Oh, Katie, poor Peg." She looked up at me, tears streaming down her cheeks.

"Aye," I said, "Poor Peg." I pulled the cloth from my pocket to wipe Elizabeth's tears. The book of maps fell to the floor with a plop.

Miss Pratt sailed into the kitchen. "Miss Elizabeth, you mustn't carry on so. You will have a setback. March straight upstairs to your room while I have a word with Mrs Plumley."

Elizabeth swiped her hand across her nose and, head bent, left the kitchen. She looked smaller and frailer since her illness, and she didn't seem to have as much fight. She obeyed Miss Pratt's every order without a word. Pray God she'd get her pluck back as she got stronger. I went to the sink to wash the Boston Marrow squash and the potatoes Mrs Plumley had set out.

"Mrs Plumley," Miss Pratt said, "I want a word with you about the dinner party Mr Pierce is planning."

Mrs Plumley stood at the stove, browning chunks of meat in fat. Without looking at Miss Pratt, she said, "Yes, Miss, Mr Pierce told me about it."

"Very good. Tomorrow I'll plan the menu with you. Mr Pierce wants everything to be just so. Now, perhaps, that the unfortunate incident with Peg is over . . ."

Anger roared through me like a windstorm. "Unfortunate incident?" I cried. "Ach, you have no heart at all, always worrying about yourself – you and your iced juice!"

Miss Pratt's eyes narrowed. Her jaw tightened. "Now, Mrs Plumley," she repeated icily, "that the unfortunate incident is over, I hope you will be able to get the household running smoothly again. I am certain Mr Pierce will be looking for a new hired girl."

Thoughts of Peg sent me past caring what Pratt the *rat* thought. I placed the vegetables on the chopping-board. Now, I grabbed the meat cleaver and slashed the squash in two. Without pausing to clean away the seeds, I hacked it into small pieces.

Mrs Plumley gaped. I caught her lips curling in a grim smile.

Miss Pratt stepped back. "Did you hear me, Mrs Plumley?" she asked, glaring at me.

Mrs Plumley turned her attention to the sizzling meat. "I heard you."

128

"Very good, Mrs Plumley." As Miss Pratt turned to leave, her foot sent the book of maps skidding across the floor. "What is this?" she said, picking it up. "What are you doing with Miss Elizabeth's book, Katie? You took it from her room, didn't you? What else have you stolen from her?"

I stared at Miss Pratt. Da's warning not to bungle my second chance rang in my ears.

She eyed me coldly. "Well, Katie, what have you to say for yourself? What else have you stolen?"

"I didn't steal anything," I flashed, looking her straight in the eye. "Elizabeth loaned the book to me when my brother went out west."

The skin around her nose whitened. "A likely story! You have been given too much liberty in this house, but you will not get away with thievery. I have put up with you long enough. Out of the kindness of my heart, because of your illness, I did not mention the scorched petticoat to Mr Pierce, and I have tried to ignore your rude tongue. But when Mr Pierce learns how you have been stealing . . ." She stopped and pulled in a deep breath. "I think, Mrs Plumley, that Mr Pierce will be hiring two new girls."

Mrs Plumley shook the wooden spoon at Miss Pratt. "You need not worry about the dinner Mr Pierce is planning for Mrs Winthrop, the pretty widow he's been courting. Katie and I will do him proud."

My mouth fell open and I dropped the cleaver onto the table.

Miss Pratt paled as she looked from me to Mrs Plumley. "What did you say?"

"I said you need not worry about the dinner."

"No, about courting? Mr Pierce? Mrs Winthrop?"

"That's right. Mrs Reilly, the wash lady, heard from Mrs

O'Neill, Mrs Winthrop's cook, that Mr Pierce spends a mighty lot of time there."

Miss Pratt lifted her chin. "That means nothing. You know very well that Mr Pierce and the late Mr Winthrop were business partners. I'm sure Mr Pierce meets with Mrs Winthrop on business."

Mrs Plumley shrugged a plump shoulder. "Not according to Mrs O'Neill. They were friends as well as partners, you know. Mrs Winthrop and the late Mrs Pierce were very close." She moved the pan from the heat and added, "Mrs Winthrop's a real lady."

Miss Pratt's face turned livid. Breathing hard, she spat out the words, "*Gossip. Lies and gossip,*" and flew from the kitchen.

22

Departure

"Send these muffins on up, Katie. Then we'll have a bit of breakfast ourselves." Mrs Plumley handed me a plate of corn muffins hot from the oven. I took them to the butler's pantry and pulled on the dumb-waiter rope to signal Thomas. My stomach jiggled with nerves. For the past few weeks, I'd been expecting a call to Mr Pierce's office. This morning Thomas told us that last night at the dinner party, Mr Pierce had announced his and Mrs Winthrop's engagement. He said that Miss Pratt's mouth had opened and closed like a fish, that her face had flushed scarlet, then gone white. Now Mr Pierce, Elizabeth and Miss Pratt were breakfasting. I wondered if this would be the morning Miss Pratt would say I'd stolen Elizabeth's books.

I sat at the table and looked at my plate of fried eggs and sausages. "Oh, Mrs Plumley, I don't know that I can eat a thing," I said. "Miss Pratt must be in an awful state."

Mrs Plumley forked eggs into her mouth. "Humph. What if she is? She deserves it. Imagine! Her thinkin' Mr Pierce would marry the likes of her!"

"But her being disappointed and all – she'll be meaner

131

than ever and deviling to get me in trouble! I'm wondering if she told Mr Pierce I've been stealing from Elizabeth." I pushed my egg about the plate.

Mrs Plumley slurped her tea. "Don't be worrying about that, Katie. I'm sure Mr Pierce is grateful you came back when Miss Elizabeth was taken sick."

"But if he thinks I've been taking things from Elizabeth . . ."

We both looked up as Thomas's precise step sounded on the stairs. He walked to the table, sat down and filled a plate.

Mrs Plumley slapped her hands on the table. "All right, Thomas. Out with it. What's going on up there?"

Thomas took his time chewing a piece of sausage. At last he said, "It is a very strange atmosphere in the dining-room this morning. Miss Elizabeth bubbles with excitement. She goes on and on about the things Mrs Winthrop has told her they will do together. Miss Pratt does not look pleased. She asked Mr Pierce for a private conference this morning." He looked at me, his forehead creased in a worried frown. "Mr Pierce said he would see her in his office immediately following breakfast. After he and Miss Elizabeth left the room, Miss Pratt said to me, 'Tell the kitchen girl that her behaviour shall be exposed.'"

The little food I had swallowed formed a hard lump in the pit of my stomach. I couldn't face Da if I were sacked again! He'd never forgive me. I bit my lip and glanced at Mrs Plumley.

"Don't worry, Katie," she said, but I could see the worry in her own eyes.

The shed door rattled and Mrs Reilly burst into the kitchen followed by a blast of cold air. "Good mornin' to ye all," she cried. "Katie, have ye got the water heatin'?"

I nodded. "I'll be right there to help you, Mrs Reilly," I said, clearing the dishes.

In the laundry room Mrs Reilly scrubbed the clothes so fast and furious that the splashing water drenched her, me and the floor. She was so excited her mouth flew as fast as her pointy elbows. "Faith, Katie, can ye believe it, child? 'Tis my last washday here. Come next week I'll be in Charlestown. Busy as always but I'll be in charge. Sure I'll be workin' hard, taking in fancy ironing for the high and mighty, and caring for my boarders. Two I'll have, a Mr Sullivan and his son. Good Irishmen from Bantry, home of the Sullivan's. Ach, Katie, put a smile on yer face. You and yer da will be comin' to me party to celebrate an Irish moving up in the world. Would that I could buy the house outright. Maybe someday women will be able to own property, but this is the next best thing. We'll have a fiddler there and Joey Mulligan with his accordion and yer da, he'll pipe a tune or two on his tin whistle."

"It sounds grand, Mrs Reilly," I said, not wanting to worry her. I sloshed the clothes in water so cold my hands ached. Then I prepared them for the drying closet.

She stopped her frantic scrubbing for a minute and gazed off. "Back in Ireland, when a man bought his own piece of land, there'd be a celebration to beat the devil. A grand *céilí*. 'Tis a great occurrence when an Irish comes to be an owner, not havin' a landlord to grab the fruit of his labour. I'll have a landlord still, but he's a fair man – and Irish to boot." She snatched up a shirt and rubbed it furiously.

I heard Thomas's step quicker than usual on the stairs. My heart quivered. I reached for a towel to dry my hands. "I . . . I think Thomas has come for me, Mrs Reilly."

Mrs Reilly stared at me.

I heard Mrs Plumley cry out, "Ah, Thomas! What news do ye have?"

My heart thumping against my ribs, I walked through the hall. Mrs Reilly, dripping suds, was right behind me.

Mrs Plumley stood near the sink. "Here's Katie and Mrs Reilly. Now, Thomas, stop standing there looking like the cat that swallowed the canary. Tell us what's happened!"

Thomas's straight shoulders straightened a little more. "You can all be well assured that I do not eavesdrop on Mr Pierce's private conversations. But this morning when Miss Pratt went into his office, I happened to be searching for something in the closet right outside the door. I couldn't help but overhear part of their conversation for their voices rose and fell. I must say, Miss Pratt sounded not at all like the proper Englishwoman she purports to be."

"On with it! On with it, man!" Mrs Plumley growled.

"Patience. Patience, my dear Mrs Plumley." Thomas cleared his throat. Looking at me, he said, "She made reference to you, Katie. I heard her talk of a scorched petticoat and you letting Miss Elizabeth handle a blazing hot iron. I couldn't hear Mr Pierce's reply. Then she called you a thief. She said he may not be worried about his daughter working like a kitchen girl, but the example you set by stealing from her was deplorable. She told him that she had seen with her own eyes one of Miss Elizabeth's books fall from your pocket."

Mrs Reilly wrung her bony hands together and the tip of her long nose reddened. "What? What's this? Katie a thief? Ridiculous!"

Thomas sniffed. "It would seem that Mr Pierce agrees with you, Mrs Reilly. He told Miss Pratt that Miss Elizabeth had told him that she had loaned Katie the book and that Katie shared her own few books with her. He said that if Miss Elizabeth wanted to loan Katie books he had no objection to it."

All the tight wires in my body relaxed and my knees

turned to jelly. I wasn't going to be sacked again! Thank the Lord, I thought, crossing myself.

Mrs Plumley placed her hands on the ledge of her stomach and chuckled. Mrs Reilly pursed her lips and bobbed her head. "I knew from the day I met the child on the docks that she'd do her da proud."

My mouth dropped open and I stared at her.

"Ye needn't look so surprised, Katie O'Brien. I'm a good judge of character, I am."

Thomas cleared his throat. "He also said that Dr Hawkins told him that Katie was a much better nurse to Miss Elizabeth than Miss Pratt herself."

Mrs Plumley gave my arm a proud poke and Mrs Reilly beamed.

"There is more," Thomas said, stifling a smile.

We all looked at him, waiting. He coughed, drew in a breath and announced, "Miss Pratt is leaving the household."

Mrs Plumley's mouth formed a perfect O. "You mean he sacked her?"

"No, he did not. Miss Pratt's voice rose considerably. You might even say she shouted at him." Thomas rolled his eyes. "She said, 'I can't stay in such a household. If you intend to do nothing about that girl, Katie O'Brien, and she is to stay on, then I must leave your employ.'"

Mrs Plumley, Mrs Reilly and I didn't move. I hardly breathed. Mrs Reilly leaned forward and said, "And what did Mr Pierce say?"

Thomas sniffed. "He said, 'You are resigning, Miss Pratt? Please allow yourself time to find another position. I will, of course, write a recommendation for you.'"

"The good Lord's sake," Mrs Plumley muttered, plumping down onto a chair.

"There's more," Thomas said, his mouth turning up at the corners. "Miss Pratt's next words were most shocking. She said, 'I will leave today. I bloody well see no reason to stay here a moment longer.' She charged out the door so fast she nearly knocked me over. Then she flew up to her room. A moment later, Mr Pierce came out and told me to hire a coach for Miss Pratt. That she would be leaving this morning."

We all looked at each other in stunned silence. Then Mrs Plumley popped up from her chair. She grabbed Mrs Reilly's and my hands and pulled us around in a jig.

I pictured Peg hooting in heaven. I couldn't help chanting, "Good riddance to *Pratt the rat!*" Mrs Plumley, her chins wobbling and her cap bobbing, and Mrs Reilly, her long face glowing and her eyes sparkling, joined me.

Thomas smiled, he actually smiled, and called over his shoulder, "I must see to the hackney."

The coach arrived mid-morning. Mrs Plumley and I stood in the hallway and listened to the commotion in the foyer above. Doors opened and shut. Thomas and the cab driver carried and bumped Miss Pratt's trunk down the stairs and out to the waiting carriage. When the front door slammed once more, Mrs Plumley and I hurried to the laundry room and peered out the street-level window. I caught a glimpse of Miss Pratt climbing into the coach. She sat by the window, staring straight ahead. The driver flicked his whip over the horse's rump and the coach lumbered into motion. "Oh, Mrs Plumley," I said, "wouldn't it be grand if Peg could see this day."

Before we were back in the kitchen, Elizabeth flew down the stairs. "Katie," she called, "Miss Pratt's gone. Papa says he will look for a new governess. But I don't need a governess."

She clapped her hands and twirled around. "Oh, I'm so happy. Miss Pratt's gone."

Thomas's step sounded on the stairs. "Mrs Plumley," he said, coming into the kitchen. "Mr Pierce would like to talk with you in his office."

"You tend to paring vegetables for the stew, Katie," she said, tucking wisps of hair under her cap. "I imagine Mr Pierce wants to tell me of the new arrangements."

Elizabeth stood at my elbow chattering away while I scraped potatoes. "Just think, Katie, Mrs Winthrop's going to be my mother."

"That's lovely," I said, smiling.

Elizabeth twirled a long brown curl and a frown creased her forehead. "Do you think she'll like me? Miss Pratt always says I'm such a bother."

Suddenly realizing how alone she must feel, I dropped the paring knife and potato with a thump and clatter and bent down to hug her. Tears stung my eyes.

Clinging to me, she whispered, "Do you think I'll be a good daughter, Katie?"

"Hush. Hush, Elizabeth. You'll be wonderful. When your father marries Mrs Winthrop, the three of you will be a real family."

A real family. Oh, where were Mam and Patrick now? I wondered. And where was Michael?

23

A Visit with Da

Later that day, I left the park and crossed the street to the alley. My mouth kept curving up as I thought of Mrs Plumley, Mrs Reilly and me dancing around and singing, "Good riddance to *Pratt the rat*." Then, down the alley, I saw Mrs Reilly rushing along. Why was she here at this time of day?

I stopped, suddenly not wanting to go any farther. The day of Peg's death flashed across my mind. The same prickles of dread rushed through me. I pushed my feet, one after the other to the courtyard. I pulled the shed door open, then the kitchen door. Mrs Plumley was stirring a stew. Mrs Reilly perched on the edge of a chair. When she saw me, she snapped to her feet. "Ach, Katie, child. 'Tis bad news I have," she said, placing her hand on a letter that lay on the table.

I couldn't breathe. I looked about the kitchen. The pattern on the red tablecloth looked sharper, the blue crockery brighter. "Michael?" I whispered.

Mrs Reilly shook her head, birdlike. "No. Not Michael. 'Tis yer brother, Patrick."

I felt lightheaded. Spots danced before me. Mrs Reilly placed her thin hands on either side of my face and gazed into my eyes. "Sit down, child. Ye look as though ye'll faint away."

Not moving, I asked, 'What's happened to Patrick?"

Mrs Reilly looked away from me. She picked up the letter. "'Tis from yer mam. Yer brother Patrick – he died, died in Cork. His strength never came back after the fever. Yer mam writes he couldn't keep a thing down. He just got weaker and weaker each day till . . ."

A howl of grief tore from my throat. "No!" I cried. "No!" I covered my face with my hands and ran sobbing to the laundry room.

Mrs Reilly followed me and put her long arms about me awkwardly. I leaned against her bony chest and cried. After a while, Mrs Reilly's small clucking noises soothed me. I stepped back from her, pressing my fingers against my eyes. She took a clean rag from the shelf and handed it to me. "Here, child, blow yer nose."

I blew my nose and wiped the tears from my face.

"Yer brother's going has changed yer mam's plans, Katie. She writes that with the money yer da and Michael sent her and with a bit of a loan from the church, she'll be sailing in November."

Mam! Coming at last. But alone. And without Patrick. "Da," I murmured. "Is Da all right?"

Mrs Reilly gave her head a quick shake. "Ach, the poor man. He's taking it hard. Losing his first–born. 'Tis a sad thing."

Yes, I thought, Da had a special fondness for Patrick. "I should go to him," I said.

"Aye, he needs comfortin'."

"Aye," Mrs Plumley agreed. "You run along. I can manage dinner without you. I'll pack something up for you to take to your da. He'll be needing some good hot food."

I watched Mrs Plumley ladle stew into a pan and secure the lid with string. I watched her wrap a loaf of bread in a towel. All the while images flashed through my mind – Maggie hurdling down to the water, Peg rattling away in a cart and Patrick – where was Patrick's last resting place?

Mrs Reilly's voice came to me through a haze. "I emptied the range and topped the coals afore I left yer da, so ye'll be able to warm the stew right away."

"Thank you," I said, tucking the bread into my skirt pocket and taking the pan from Mrs Plumley.

"God go with ye, Katie," the two women murmured as I opened the door.

Outside, an autumn breeze chilled me. The heat from the pan I carried against my chest was the only warm spot on me. Patrick dead and me going to comfort Da. It couldn't be true.

My step slowed as I approached the Granary Burying Ground on Tremont Street. I'd walked through there on fine summer days and read the inscriptions on the stones. The thought of the pictures etched on the thin gravemarkers sent chills through me – shovels, skeletons, skulls on death's swift wings. Where was Patrick now? Where was Peg? And Maggie? A feeling of heaviness – as though the burying ground were pulling me to it – filled me. I shuddered and raced so fast past the graveyard that the bread bounced against my leg and some of the gravy oozed from under the pot lid, soaking my dress. Its wetness felt like a wound in my chest.

By the time I reached Hull Street little light remained in the sky and deep shadows filled the road. I climbed the hill, trying to think what to say to Da. I ached to have Michael by my side. I'd slip my hand into his and feel safe. But now I was on my own.

I'd been here to see Da every week since Peg's death. I'd lug water in, heat it and clean the dirty room as best I could, then make tea for Da. He'd come in from the docks, drained and tired-looking. Sometimes I'd see fresh bruises on his face, sometimes older ones, yellow and fading. When I put my wages on the table, he'd nod and take all but a few pennies, insisting I keep them for myself. Taking my wages seemed to bother him. I suppose it went against his pride.

I shifted the pot, its pressure settling the cold wetness of my dress against me, and pushed open the door to our building. The smells and noise of the place choked me. A ragged little boy darted past me, chased by another ragged boy screaming, "*I'll get you! I'll get you!*"

I knocked on Da's door feeling as scared as I had back in June when Michael and I'd just arrived. No answer. Mrs O'Connor, who lived upstairs, came down the rickety steps. "Did you see my boys, Katie? Faith! Those two! Always fighting. Never give me a minute's peace."

"They just ran out, Mrs O'Connor," I said. I pushed Da's door open. "Da?" I whispered into the darkness.

"He's not there. I saw him leave right after Mrs Reilly. She told me about the death in your family. I'm sorry for it, Katie. There's too much loss in our lives. Too much." She went to the door and shouted, "Willie! Denny!" She turned and called to me, "Your da's most likely gone for a pint to ease his heartbreak."

I nodded and went into the room. It was dark but for the glow of the coal fire in the stove. I placed the pot on the table and took the bread from my pocket. I fumbled for the box of matches. I struck a match and lit the lamp. I breathed in its heavy, oily smell. The mess and clutter of the room flashed into light and cockroaches scurried for cover. My skin crawled. I shuddered and drew into myself. I took the pot to the stove and poked at the coals with the fire iron. I added a few lumps from the bucket, then took the water jug and went to the hall to fill it. While the water heated, I hung Da's few denim shirts on hooks and straightened the threadbare blanket on his cot.

I poured boiling water over tea leaves, and some into a pan. With a ragged cloth, I scrubbed the stained table. I welcomed the work, not wanting to sit down, not wanting to think about Patrick. It seemed useless though, trying to clean the place. The smells were overpowering and the cockroaches ever-present. I remembered Michael saying, 'The tenement's just wicked. The slops – people throw them into the streets. Sickness. Noise. No privacy. 'Tis no place to live.'

Michael had left. I knew it was my fault, but I knew he wanted to leave the tenement too. Over on Beacon Street, I lived much better even as a hired girl. And soon Mrs Reilly would be moving to Charlestown. Maybe Da could too. And when Mam and Patrick, . . .

Then the news about Patrick hit me in the stomach all over again. How could it be real?

The door opened and Da lurched into the room. He was unshaven and his shaggy hair fell over his eyes. He swung a bucket of ale onto the table, spilling some, pulled back a chair and sat down heavily.

I went to him and reached out to pat his shoulder, but he jerked his head up and slurred, "Pour me a mug of ale, Katie."

I wrung my hands. "There's stew heating, Da. Mrs Plumley sent it with some fresh bread. And the tea's brewing." I went to the stove and stirred the stew. "It's nice and hot, Da."

Da slapped his big hands down on the table so hard the lamp jumped and the light flickered crazily. My heart jumped and flickered with it. "I said to give me some ale, Katie. I'm not wanting stew, bread or tea. Do ye hear me?"

Trembling, I took a mug from the shelf over the sink, went to the table and dipped it full for Da. He took it and downed it fast, then dipped for another.

I went to the stove and moved the stew from the heat. I poured it into a bowl and washed the pot. My throat hurt. I tried to swallow but my mouth was dry.

I licked my lips and said, "Da, it's time I left."

Da sat at the table, staring at the oil lamp's wavering flame. A great sigh shuddered through him. "Yer mother, Katie, she'll be sailing the winter season, alone, on one of those ships. Coffin ships they call 'em. And sailing in winter, the worse time – a time of storms – storms and shipwrecks."

"Da . . ." My voice was a whisper.

Da didn't take his eyes from the flame. "Go, Katie. Go back to Beacon Street."

I took the empty pot and left.

24

The Céilí

Ientered the church a few blocks from Hull Street. It was
smoky with incense and guttering candles. I dipped my
fingers in the basin by the door, blessed myself and slid into
a pew. It was eighteen days since I'd learned that Patrick had
died, eighteen days since I'd seen Da. Soon, I would meet
him to go to Mrs Reilly's céilí, then back to the tenement to
stay overnight. The heavy knot in my stomach tightened. I
didn't want to see Da. I felt so useless. I knew I couldn't
comfort him.

Farther forward, a woman, her shawl pulled tight over her
head, murmured the rosary. The gentle click of her beads and
the quiet of the church calmed me. The old lady finished her
prayers and shuffled down the aisle. I heard the door shut
behind her and I was alone.

I looked around the church, remembering the Sundays
that Peg and I had run through the streets to attend the first
Mass of the day, then hurried back to Beacon Street. Sun
streamed through the arched windows, bathing tendrils of
smoke that rose from candles. I went to the altar and lit one
for Maggie, Peg and Patrick and bowed my head in prayer.
My muscles clenched in sudden anger. Why couldn't they

have lived, God? Why couldn't they have got better like Elizabeth and me?

Mam, I thought. The anger drained from me and I pressed my hand against my chest where the Holy Family medal had lain. Mam would be here next month. She would, I told myself, blocking out the memory of the nightmare that wouldn't leave me alone – the horrible image of Maggie's shrouded body hurdling down, down, down to icy black water.

I clasped my hands tightly and prayed real hard for Mam's safe crossing. Then Mam, Da and I would be together. No Patrick and . . . no Michael. Not a word from Michael but the one letter in September. Was he all right? I wondered. Was he even alive? Sure I would feel it in my heart if Michael were no longer on this earth. I thought of the medal round his neck. It was fitting I didn't have it. Our family would never be together again.

Outside, the afternoon was bright and calm. "Nice weather we're havin' for November," Mrs Plumley had said when I left after midday chores. She'd slipped the package of cookies she and I had baked into my hands, saying, "You take these to Mrs Reilly for her housewarming. Now be sure you're back by noon tomorrow. Mrs Winthrop and four others are coming for a late dinner."

I walked through the streets carrying the cookies carefully. My step slowed as I climbed Hull Street. At Da's door, I raised my hand to knock, then, recalling my last visit, dropped it to my side. I took a deep breath, then rapped on the door.

The door opened and Da, wearing a white shirt and clean work pants, said, "Well, here ye are, Katie. 'Tis time we were on our way." He strode to the table, picked up his tin whistle and a growler of ale.

"We'll be taking the horsecar, Katie. We could walk the

distance, but I think it fittin' we take our first trip to Charlestown in style."

I hurried up the street, struggling to keep up with Da's long-legged stride. Taking a horsecar! 'Twould cost at least two cents apiece. What was Da thinking of?

We waited at a busy corner. Carriages and two-seaters rumbled by and people darted from one side of the street to the other. I sneaked a look at Da. He was whistling a tune just like Michael always did. He looked down at me from his great height, his bushy brows jutting over his eyes. His lips turned up in a smile, but I saw the sadness in his eyes. "Faith, Katie, we'll have a good time tonight. It's a grand occasion for Mrs Reilly."

I smiled back. I knew Da was hurting inside about Patrick and worried about Mam. So was I! But Da was acting like he was glad to see me! Maybe we could have a good time. Soon a horsecar, drawn by two grey horses, came into view. The driver pulled on the reins. The horses, snorting and shaking their heads, slowed to a stop. A picture of men on horseback decorated the side of the car.

"Up ye go, Katie," Da said.

I climbed into the car and slid into a seat. The driver yelled, "Giddap." The horses whinnied and the car lurched into motion. I settled the cookies on my lap and watched the horses' big rumps heave from side to side. The stench of fresh horse-dung rose from the road. The car swayed and bumped then made a sharp turn, throwing me against Da. His shoulder felt rock solid. I relaxed a little. I was on an outing with my da.

The horses' hooves made a hollow clip-clopping sound as they trotted over the wooden planks of the Charlestown Bridge. On the other side of the bridge, Da pointed past me.

"Look down there, Katie." My gaze followed his pointing finger to a wharf where tall masts rose above warehouses. "There's work over here for a man if they'll hire an Irish. But there's too many men and not enough jobs," he muttered.

"Do you think you might find work here, Da? Then when Mam comes . . ." I stopped, seeing Da's fierce look.

He scowled at the rolling ocean. "Pray to God, she has a safe journey, Katie."

Both of us fell quiet.

"Here's where we get off," he said at the first stop past the bridge.

I clambered down the steps and we walked through narrow cobbled roads. The street lamps glowed dimly in the dusk. Finally, Da stopped in front of a two-story house, one in a row of identical houses. "This should be it," he said, knocking on the door.

"Come in, come in, Seán O'Brien, and there's Katie behind ye." Mrs Reilly, wearing a ruffled white blouse and a long black skirt, glowed. A red velvet ribbon fastened to the neck of her blouse with a tiny gold brooch added a dash of colour. She looked so different from when she came to the Pierce House in her drab work-clothes.

We stepped into a small centre hallway where a flight of stairs rose to the upper floor. In the living room to the right a man pushed and pulled on an accordion. "Hey, O'Brien, did you bring your whistle?" he called.

"Aye, Mulligan," Da said, taking his tin whistle from his pocket.

"Mrs Plumley and I made these for the party," I said, handing Mrs Reilly the cookies.

"Thank ye, Katie, and give me thanks to Mrs Plumley. Ye can put them on the table in the dining-room," she said, nodding to the room to the left. "Then get yerself a glass of punch in the kitchen."

I unwrapped the cookies and placed them on the table full of food. It looked like everyone had brought an offering: a plate of cold meats and cheese, warm meat-pies, biscuits, cakes and fruit-pies. The kitchen smelled delicious and my stomach rumbled. I ladled a glass of punch from the bowl set in the middle of the table.

Faith, 'tis grand, I thought, looking around. The kitchen ran along the back of the house. The delicious smell came from a kettle simmering on the coal stove. I wondered if there was an ice chest and opened the back door. Sure enough, there it was in a corner of the small porch.

Mrs Reilly's voice startled me. "So, Katie, me girl, how do ye like it?"

I closed the door and came back into the warm kitchen. The sounds of the accordion and Da's whistle filled the house. "'Tis grand, Mrs Reilly. I wish my Mam could live in such a place."

Mrs Reilly pinched the tip of her long nose and took a deep breath. "In truth, Katie, I'm thinkin' the same. I told yer Da I've two rooms to let. One is spoke for but t'other's empty. 'Twould be grand if yer mam and da could take it. 'Tis a good-sized room, big enough for the three of ye."

"What about Michael?"

"Michael?"

"When he comes back?"

Mrs Reilly looked away from me. "Aye. We'd find a spot for Michael." She went to the stove to stir the kettle. "'Tis a hearty fish stew to fill their bellies. What with all the ale flowing in there I don't want any drunkenness."

"Oh, Mrs Reilly, if only Da could find work here in Charlestown!"

"I've said the same to him, but he says nothin' 'bout his thoughts to me. Now run to the other room and enjoy yerself."

The warm, smoky room smelled of people and drink. They shouted and laughed over the sound of the music. Someone called out, "Hey, Mulligan, give us a reel. 'Tis time for a little soft shoe."

A heavy woman shouted encouragement and pushed a chair against the wall.

Soon the man called Mulligan was playing a snappy tune. Toes tapped and heads wagged and, suddenly, Mrs Reilly was dancing. She lifted her skirt above her ankles and her skinny legs flew in time to the music. Her feet skimmed the wooden boards, stepping, pointing, crossing over and back, hopping and jumping. Then Da stepped out beside her. His heavy steps made the windows rattle and the candles flicker.

I joined the others, clapping to the rhythm. Watching Da brought back a long forgotten memory, him teaching Michael, Patrick and me the Irish dances. Patrick had caught on right away. But Patrick would dance no more. The thought made me feel lonely, set apart. I sighed and went to the kitchen. A minute later Da came out, his face red and sweaty. He blew the spit out of his whistle and wiped it clean. Not saying a word, he poured a mug of ale from a pitcher and downed it. He placed the empty glass on the table and rubbed his eyes. I wondered if he was thinking about Patrick, too.

A man and a boy not much older than me came in from the dining room. The boy crammed a meat-pie into his mouth. The man poured himself a tankard of ale, asking, "Do ye hear anything from yer boy, O'Brien?"

"Not for a time now," Da said.

"God be with him. I know a woman heard news her husband was killed in a riot in one of those rough railroad towns. Several Irish lads lost their lives."

My heart stopped and I glanced at Da. He frowned and drew his pipe and tobacco pouch from a pocket. "Nice spot you and yer boyo have here with Maggie Reilly," he said, packing his pipe.

"Aye, Johnny and me like it here, don't we, Johnny?"

Johnny nodded, his mouth too full to speak.

Mr Sullivan thrust his chin at me. "This your girl?"

"Aye," Da said. "Katie, my daughter."

"Pretty little colleen," Mr Sullivan said, winking at me. "She'll grow into a right beauty."

I felt my face burning and picked up the ladle for something to do. "Aye," I heard Da say. "A looker with a head for learning. She wants to go to school. But I don't trust the public schools what with all their Protestant ways."

Mr Sullivan pointed his tankard at his son. "Johnny there's going to school. He pays no mind to them adding on to the Lord's prayer and such. He studies the books, eh, Johnny? And works part-time to help out."

"Mmph," Da muttered. He slid a look at me from under his ledge of brows. "Maybe it can be done."

His words soared through me like a rainbow through the sky and my heart sang. Was Da thinking to agree with me about school?

Johnny Sullivan, dark blue eyes twinkling, took the ladle from my hand and poured me a glass of punch. He then poured himself one and washed down the meat-pie. He set the empty glass down and asked, "Can ye do a jig, Katie?"

Da struck a match for his pipe. "Course she can. Didn't I, myself, teach her?"

Johnny took my hand and led me to the living-room where the whine of a fiddle had joined the accordion. My face felt as hot as the simmering kettle on the stove. I stumbled a few times, but soon the steps came back to me and I danced. Not like Mrs Reilly, but I danced.

After a time, Mulligan squeezed his accordion shut and went to the dining-room to fill a plate. I saw Da disappear into the kitchen, then come back with another pint. The fiddler, a thin man with eyes as dark and big as a fawn's, stroked a few notes and hummed a tune. A woman called out, "Danny, give us a song!"

Others echoed her. Danny bowed his fiddle, closed his eyes and sang beautiful and sad love songs. Johnny sang snatches of "Believe Me If All Those Endearing Young Charms" with him. The room grew quiet and the faces around me looked sad and longing. Someone handed Danny a glass of ale. He wet his throat, tightened a string, then stroked the opening bars to "Molly Malone". Each time he sang "Molly Malone" I heard Michael singing, "Katie O'". I thought of him singing to me on the dock when we arrived and again in the park. Danny ended the song with a whispery high "Cockles and mussels". A great sadness filled me.

I left Johnny singing along with the others and went into the dining-room. A woman had just arrived and placed a bowl of spicy smelling onions on the table. I took a few empty plates to the kitchen. Mrs Reilly was tasting the stew. Perspiration beaded her forehead and she smelled faintly of soap. "Faith, 'tis time to set this out," she said. "Will ye clear a spot on the dining-room table for me, Katie?"

As I rearranged dishes on the table, the strains of "Kathleen Mavourneen" drifted from the living-room. Images of Ireland filled my head – the deep blue lough, the emerald green hills. When Danny sang the chorus other voices chimed in: "*Mavourneen, Mavourneen, my sad tears are falling, To think that from Erin and thee I must part, It may be for years, and it may be forever . . .*" I stood in the dining-room listening to the voices grow husky. I guessed most everyone there had people back in Ireland and was wondering, when or will I see them again? I thought of Mam's dangerous voyage and shivered with fear.

A man called out, "Best ye all stop dreamin' of Ireland. There's nothin' but tears for the Irish there."

"Faith, things ain't much better here, what with all the 'Irish Need Not Apply' signs." Uneasy, I moved to the hallway and looked in. The music stopped and men, sweaty and red-faced, eyed each other warily.

Danny, the fiddler, spoke up. "Have ye heard that Séamus O'Donnell speak? Now he makes sense. Talks about the power of the people. Says 'tis only through voting we'll get our own men in."

A bearded man, called O'Casey, stuck out his chin and glared at Da. "Then there's those think we should stay 'mongst ourselves, like Dennis O'Malley's United Irish."

"I don't hold with that bunch," Mrs Reilly piped in from the kitchen doorway.

"Eh, Aggie Reilly, here ye are – a woman – and always puttin' yer two cents worth in."

Laughter floated through the room.

"You just wait!" she said, shaking a long finger. "One day we women will have the right to vote. And 'tis my 'pinion that the United Irish are naught but thugs!"

Several men agreed.

"Aye. Yer right there."

"Fools! That's what they are."

Mrs Reilly nodded. She thrust her chin towards the dining-room. "Now get yerselves in there and fill yer bellies."

Most of the women and a few of the men started toward the dining-room. They stopped when O'Casey's challenging words rang out. "What about you, Seán O'Brien? I've seen ye with O'Malley."

The room went quiet.

Da, his colour high, said in a low, angry voice, "A man's entitled to his own views, O'Casey."

O'Casey's jaw jutted out. "Don't want to say, eh?"

Da looked round the room, his brows drawn together.

Breathless, I waited for Da's answer.

"I have this to say. We Irish need to stick together so's we can pass our heritage on to our children." He glanced at me. "But a man can change his mind as to how that can be done."

"So, are ye saying ye've nothing to do with that crowd, O'Brien?" O'Casey pressed..

Da narrowed his eyes. "Those of ye that work with me down on the wharf – ye know I speak up for what I think's right. When I fight, I fight fair and square, for myself and mine. With my fists. No guns. No knives."

"That doesn't sound like O'Malley's group," a sallow-faced man called.

"'Tis what I've found out," Da admitted. "And 'tis 'cause of that that Dennis O'Malley and I 'ave parted ways."

O'Casey seemed to ponder Da's words. "So what are ye saying, O'Brien? That we should become naturalized citizens – get the right to vote?"

Wide-eyed, I stared at Da.

A loud hammering at the front door pulled my eyes from Da. The door swung open. A man stuck his head in and shouted, "Fire! Across the Charles."

25

Fire

Outside, the sky across the Charles glowed red. I pulled my wrap round me against the chill air and hurried to keep up with Da's long stride. Doors opened and people crying *"Fire!"* flowed into the street.

At the bridge, Da stopped dead. I caught up to him and stared across the river.

"Jesus, Mary and Joseph," Da murmured, "that's some blaze. Looks like the business centre this time."

The smell of smoke, the glow of sky – an image of Ireland – huts burning, people fleeing – Mam and Patrick – flashed through my mind.

Da merged with the crowd running across the bridge. I followed. People sped by, their faces an eerie blur in the sky's glow. We ran on. Curls of smoke filled the air and set me to coughing.

Voices rang out *"Fire!"*

"The stores are burning!"

"All those goods going up in smoke!"

Alarm bells pealed. Suddenly, the crowd jammed to a stop. Police shoved us back and shouted through brass horns,

"Make room for the engine. Make room." Horses pulled an engine filled with firemen dressed in bright red jackets and black trousers.

I squeezed next to Da.

A police man right in front of us raised his horn and bellowed, *"Stand back! Stand back!* A building's about to blow!"

Everyone grew quiet as the building began to sway. Its upper stone front wobbled outward. Then, with a thundering crash, it collapsed.

The mob whooped.

Stunned, I stared at the wasteland beyond the fallen building. Skeletal structures still burning. Thick smoke spiralling upwards. Flaming sparks and cinders flying like brilliant birds. In the distance, church steeples glowing red, ships – black silhouettes.

A man near us breathed, "Holy Mother! The city's half gone."

Then, *"The fire's spreading!"*

"Firemen can't control it . . ."

"Heading for the tenements . . ."

Ragged, soot-blackened men, women and children, carrying armloads of coats, shoes and boots, dodged the police, nearly knocking us over.

A giant voice boomed out, "Goods for the taking."

The crowd moved as one huge monster. Elbows jabbed me. Hands thrust me away. Boots stomped on my feet.

The heavy, hot smell of sweat and fear suffocated me. My clothes stuck to me. Da's strong hands dug into my shoulders and half dragged me out of the surging mob. A brisk breeze blew. My overheated body began to shiver.

Da coughed and spat into the street. "The wind's fanning

the fire right towards the tenements, Katie. If our place goes up . . ." He shook his head and pressed his hands against his face.

"What, Da? What is it?"

"Ah, Katie. I've stashed my earnings in the cup. 'Tis all I've got. You go on back to Beacon Street. Ye'll be safe there." He turned and loped away.

I ran after him.

He stopped and glared down at me. "Katie, listen to me. Get on over to Beacon Street."

"But, Da," my voice came in short gasps, "there's Mr and Mrs O'Connor and little Will and Denny and the new family just moved into Mrs Reilly's room and all the others. I've got to see they're all right!"

"Ach, ye'll be the death of me yet." He squinted at the chaos around us. "Looks like the fire's jumped over towards Hanover. The firemen – they're keeping it from Faneuil Hall and Quincy Market. They'll pay no mind to the tenements." Da started off again, me right behind him.

We hastened down past Faneuil Hall and Quincy Market to the waterfront. People, still in their nightclothes, poured from the narrow streets and alleys of the North End. Some screaming, some wide-eyed and silent, children wailing and stumbling after their parents, children lost – crying for their mams. And fleeter than all were the rats, scurrying from the flames, finding refuge along the warehouses on the waterfront.

Da and I took a roundabout route towards Hull Street. We paused for breath at the Old North Church. Patches of fire brightened the sky behind us and smoke and cinders drifted by.

"Look, Da. It's stopped. It hasn't crossed Hanover."

"The wind's changed direction, thank the good Lord. The men themselves will be working to keep the flames back – getting buckets of water, drenching the streets, the houses. Ye'll not see firemen up here, Katie. If ye don't pay for the service, they'll let ye burn to the ground."

We climbed the streets at a slower rate. "I'll get my money out, then head back to help." He grabbed me by the shoulders and glared at me. "And you stay in the room. I'll not have ye out fighting a fire."

As we neared our tenement, a flaming torch arced through the air and splintered Da's window. Stealthy figures disappeared into the shadows.

Da stopped me. "Stay here!"

"Da, someone's setting fire to our place!"

"Aye. Stay here!" He sprinted up the street.

I raced after him.

Two men leapt out of a doorway and pounced on Da.

"Da! Da!" I screamed.

One of the men – Patch-eye – pinned Da's arms behind his back. Huge Spike Wood pulled his arm back and slammed his meaty fist into Da's face. The smack of the blow made me shudder.

I darted past them into the building crying, *"Help! Help!"*

Doors opened upstairs. Mr O'Connor, candle in hand, stood at the top of the stairs.

I tripped and fell half-way up. A sharp pain pierced my knee. "Da! They're beating my da," I cried.

"I'll get help," Mr O'Connor promised, disappearing into the hallway.

The smell of smoke reached me. Da's money! I hurried to our room, ignoring the pains shooting up my leg. The bedding beneath the window smouldered. I stumbled to the sink along the back wall for the bucket of cold water. In my rush, I bumped into the stove. Steamy heat rose from the pot of water Da kept there against the night chill. I picked up the cold water bucket, dashed back to the bed, sloshed the water over the smoking blankets.

A brightness in back of me. Footsteps. A chill of fear down my spine. I turned.

A man, holding a torch, kicked the door shut behind him.

Dimly, I heard footsteps pounding down the stairs, voices hollering. Mr O'Connor. Could I call out to him? Would he hear me above the din? Was Da all right?

The man said nothing. The flickering torch threw grotesque shadows across his face, red glints in his eyes.

Da's money. Da's voice, *''Tis all I've got'*.

Keeping my eyes on the torch, I edged around the table. I'd snatch Da's money from the cup above the sink, then dart to the door.

The man watched me. Like a cat with a mouse. Like in the alley that night. My heart stopped.

I was almost to the back wall.

The man stepped forward. He pointed the torch at me. "Not another step, Katie O'Brien."

I felt myself go all still inside. I backed away.

The man moved closer.

My eyes glued to the flaming torch, I moved backwards. The hard edge of the stove stopped me.

He held the torch higher. In its wavering light I saw his face. The hairs on my neck rose. I opened my mouth to scream but not a sound came out.

"Think you're seeing a ghost, do ya?" Weasel-face laughed evilly. "That scum brother of yours leaves me for dead, then high-tails it out of Boston. Thanks to him I've been laid up in the hospital all this time. Big Spike and me – we figured let the Mick think he killed me, got him out of town anyway. And we've been planning to take care of Seán O'Brien and his pretty little girl – the fire tonight gave us just the right chance."

My mind raced as fast as my heart. A long angry scar ran along Weasel-face's forehead. His left eye, the left side of his mouth, in fact, all the muscles on the left side of his face, drooped. A nasty grin twisted his mouth and showed the gaping holes of missing teeth.

I swallowed, working for spit to moisten my dry mouth. Finally able to speak, I blurted, "Michael didn't hit you. Patch-eye did. He was aiming for Michael but he hit you."

"Sure he did," he sneered, so close that I could taste his foul odor. "You've caused me a lot of trouble, little girl. But I'll put an end to that right now." He raised the torch.

I turned, grabbed the boiling pot and flung it upwards at Weasel-face. Pain seared my hands. Drops spattered, scalding me.

Weasel-face shrieked, a blood-curdling sound, his hands flew to his face, the torch to the floor. He tripped over a chair, crashed to the floor.

I pulled mugs from the shelf till I found Da's money. I stuffed it in my pocket.

Hair-raising screams rent the air.

I turned.

Weasel-face, all aflame, floundered from the room, fanning the flames that seared him. He had fallen on his torch.

I ran screaming into the hall. A man, carrying a bucket of water from the back hall, dashed by me and into the room.

Out on the street, a man shrugged out of his coat, threw

it over Weasel-face and wrested him to the ground. Another flew from a building with a pail of water, doused him with it. The flames hissed and died.

Men were coming from their buildings with buckets of water. Women and children gathered in small groups, gazing at the nightmarish scene.

"Da! Da! Where are you?"

"Katie," Mrs O'Connor, called from a doorway. "Yer Da's over here."

Sobs choking me I ran to Da.

Mr O'Connor knelt by his side. "He's hurt bad."

Da lay on the cobbled stones, his eyes swollen shut, blood covering his face. Fresh blood flowed from a knife wound on his arm.

I lay against him shaking and crying.

26

Running for Help

"Ach, Katie." Da's eyes fluttered open and he struggled to sit up. He coughed and spat blood. Grunting, he staggered to his feet.

Mr O'Connor grasped one of his arms. I seized the other. Together, we held him up.

"Where can we go?" I asked. "Our room's all smoky. The bed's soaking wet."

"Our place," Mrs O'Connor offered.

"My own room," Da said, his voice cracking with weariness and pain.

Mrs O'Connor protested. "But Katie says 'tis . . ."

"My room." Da insisted in a thin whisper.

Mr O'Connor nodded to his wife. "Ready his room, Molly. 'Tis where he wants to be."

By the time we reached our room, Mrs O'Connor and two other women had taken Da's bedding out and replaced it with a thin mattress and some worn blankets. Da, breathing hard, fell onto the bed.

"I can tend him," I said. "Thank you all kindly for your help."

"I'd stay with ye, Katie, but me boys they're real upset they are. They'll be needing me," Mrs O'Connor whispered. "But give a holler if ye need me, hear?"

I nodded and Mr and Mrs O'Connor left.

I was alone with Da. His arm bled something fierce and the syrupy fluid soaked into the bedding. I searched for towels to stem the bleeding and to clean Da's wounds but could find nothing but tattered rags. I thought of all the clean linens neatly stacked in closets at the Pierce house and of Dr Hawkins. Oh, how I wished I could run across the street for Dr Hawkins!

I tugged my petticoat down, ripped a strip off and wrapped it tight around Da's deep cut. His cry of pain shivered through me. What if I was doing more harm than good? My hands had blistered from grabbing the pot of hot water. Ignoring the pain, I poked at the coals to fire them, then took a kettle and went for water to heat, all the time praying, "Please, God, don't let Da die, too."

I set the kettle on the stove and topped the coals. While the water warmed, I went to Da. A heavy stench of blood rose from him. His swollen eyes were blackening. Trails of sticky blood oozed from his nose. The skin over his left cheekbone was split open. His breath rattled in his chest. When the water warmed, I carried it to Da's bed and dipped strips of my torn petticoat in it.

I unwrapped the blood-soaked rag on his arm. The bleeding seemed to be slowing some but started up fresh when I washed the deep gash. Da groaned. His eyes flickered open, then shut. I took one of his clean work shirts from a hook, folded it into a pad and bound it in place with a strip of petticoat, then cleaned his face. He turned his head away. "Leave me be, Katie. Leave me be." Then he fell into a deep sleep. Air whistled through his open mouth and his chest rose and fell quickly as he laboured for breath.

"Da! Da!" I cried. But his eyes didn't open and he didn't answer me.

In the shadow of the unsteady light, his face grew white and waxy under splotches of dark and drying blood. Could he be bleeding inside like the man back home who'd been kicked by a mule? That man had died. Da couldn't die. He couldn't!

If only Dr Hawkins were here! He'd make Da well.

I paced about the room, the boards creaking under my feet. I ran my hands through my wild hair. I had to get Dr Hawkins! Sure and Da didn't want charity, but I had my earnings. We could pay, we could. I stood over Da and listened to his troubled breathing. Moving quickly, I covered him with a blanket, snuffed the light and clambered upstairs to tell Mrs O'Connor I was going for the doctor. Could she look in on Da?

Outside, I ran through the deserted streets to Hanover and on to Scollay Square. Fire blazed in patches through the smouldering city. I raced on to Tremont Street, passing a few lone people hurrying toward the smoky streets, others, carrying goods, hurrying away. The hair on my neck prickled when I neared the cemeteries. I hated passing them at night for Mrs Plumley had filled my head with tales of roaming spirits.

The gravestones in the Granary Burying Ground reflected a ghostly light. A figure loomed in the cemetery gate. It lurched out and grabbed my arm. My throat went dry and my heart raced. It was no ghost that had me but a man who stank of drink. I struggled to get away. He bent close to my face. Spittle spraying, he garbled, "'Tis the end of the world! Like the Bible says – All's going up in flame."

"Let me go!" I twisted free. "Jesus, Mary, and Joseph," I cried, crossing myself as I pelted on toward the Common, pain stabbing my sore knee. A horse-drawn fire engine rumbled past me.

People milled about the park. I caught snatches of phrases: " . . . store's gone, burned to the ground." Cuss words. A cry of " . . . build again!" I dashed through the crowd. Smoke choked me and stung my eyes. At Arlington Street I turned right and sprinted past the alley to Beacon Street. Dr Hawkins had to come. He had to!

Panting, I climbed the steps to his brownstone house and hammered on the door. I pounded again and again, the sound echoing my heart pounding against my ears. My head ached and my throat scratched. My blistered hands felt twice their usual size. Where was Dr Hawkins?

After a time, the door opened. An elegant-looking woman wearing a silky blue robe, said, "What is it, child?"

I tried to speak but could do nothing but cough. When the cough left me, I cleared my throat and, in a hoarse whisper, said, "Please, Ma'am, I must see Dr Hawkins."

"I'm sorry but my husband isn't here. He's helping out at the fire," Mrs Hawkins said, moving to close the door.

"Please, Ma'am," I begged. "He must come to my Da. He's bleeding, and . . ."

I choked back the tears clogging my throat. Pulling myself up, I thrust my chin out. "I can pay. I work across the street at the Pierce House. I can pay with my next wages."

Voices and steps sounded along the walk. I looked down and saw Dr Hawkins, sooty and hunched over, with his butler. "Dr Hawkins," I cried. "Please, you must come for my da. Two men beat him something terrible! He's white as a ghost and I can't wake him!"

"Why, it's Katie O'Brien," he said. "What's happened to you? You're covered with blood!"

"'Tis my da's blood. He's hurt. Please come. I can pay, Dr Hawkins. I'm not asking for charity. My da won't take charity. I won't take charity. I can pay."

"Calm down, Katie," he said, placing a hand on my shoulder. "Where is your father?"

"Over on Hull Street."

Dr Hawkins turned to his butler. "Matthew, run to the stables and bring my two-seater round." He looked at me. Dark circles ringed his kind eyes. "While Matthew's getting the carriage we've time to bathe those hands and put some salve on them. Then, Katie, we'll go to your father."

27

Things Look Up

Weasel-face died in November fire – Stop –
Not in Alley – Stop – Da hurt bad – Stop –
Come home – Stop – Spike Wood and Patch-eye
disappeared – Stop – Katie

The telegraph I'd wired to Michael, care of the railroad, two weeks ago, played through my mind as I walked toward the Common. Would they reach him? Would he come home? Was he all right?

A breeze carrying the hint of snow and the lingering haze of the fire blew across the park. For a week or more after the fire, piles of coal had smouldered and filled the air with black smoke, and every so often flames had blazed out from hot embers. I could still smell smoke. The tiniest trace of it tightened my nerves. I scooted along a path, in a hurry to get to Da's. I'd been visiting him every day since that terrifying night.

The park was full of stalls where merchants sold what they had saved from the fire. I pulled my coat close against the cold and waved to Thomas, who was minding Mr Pierce's stall. Mr Pierce's stores had burned to the ground. Now Pierce House was busy with men coming and going, making plans to rebuild.

I stopped at a temporary food stand. I was buying stew beef, potatoes and carrots to make a meal for Da and me when Mr O'Donnell grasped my shoulder and said, "Well, Katie O'Brien, I'm delighted to find you out and about on this crisp autumn day. I suspect that you are on your way to visit your da?"

"Oh, Mr O'Donnell, how are you?" I cried looking up into his sparkling eyes, bluer than ever in his wind-reddened face.

"I'm fine, Katie." He raised his brows and his eyes twinkled. "And, you'll be happy to hear – I'll soon be teaching a class."

"Teaching? You've been hired on as a teacher?"

He shook his head. "No. I'm afraid it will be years before we Irish are teaching in the public schools. But I've found as I urge newcomers to become citizens that many would like to learn to read. They want to better themselves – to move up in the world."

"So you'll be teaching grown-ups?"

"Some, and their children, too. Ah, the magic of words, Katie. They transport us to other lands. They open new worlds to us." Smiling, he asked, "And how is the Shakespeare coming?"

"'Tis wonderful, Mr O'Donnell. 'Tis everything you always said. I'm reading *Romeo and Juliet* now."

"One of my favourites. But tell me, how are you faring, Katie?" He took my hands and turned them over. "Ah, they are healing nicely." He dropped them and studied my face. "But you are looking thin and peaked. You are worried about your mother's crossing. You and your da, too."

I nodded. "Aye. The paper warns about cholera on the ships. Says there's a greater risk of it during the winter what with rough weather and the cold and damp. And Thomas tells me all sorts of things about the packet ships. He said the owners are only interested in making money, that the captains have to keep to schedule no matter what. And you know, Mr O'Donnell how they crowd us on. Our journey was bad enough, but my mam, sailing now . . ." I looked up at him for reassurance, but he looked away and took my package from the shopkeeper.

He fell into step with me. "We made the journey safely, Katie. Remember that."

We walked on in silence. When we passed the telegraph office, I said, "Can you believe, Mr O'Donnell, how all those little signals of dots and dashes mean something? 'Tis like a miracle."

"Aye, Katie. I'd venture to guess that the future holds many miraculous changes – if not in my time, then in yours."

"You know, Mr O'Donnell," I hesitated. It didn't seem right, talking about my da, but I wanted Mr O'Donnell to know how I felt.

"Yes, Katie?"

"My da's changed so. And I think it's because of you. When I'm with him, he talks about the things you and he talk about when you visit him. I think he's planning to become a citizen so's he can vote. Truly, the change in him is another miracle!"

Mr O'Donnell laughed and handed me the food package. "I'll leave you here, Katie, I've a meeting to attend." He gripped my shoulders and looked down into my eyes. "If a miracle's been at work on your da, I'd say it was you, Katie O'Brien."

I stared after his tall form as he strode down the street. A little happy glow lit my insides.

By the time I reached Hull Street, my hands and feet were chunks of ice. I ducked my head to avoid the wind tunnelling up between the buildings and blowing right through my coat. Just as I reached Da's tenement, the door opened and Da stepped out. His face, all shades of black and blue, was thinner. But he looked much better than he had the night Dr Hawkins went to see him. And he was alive!

"Da, where are you going?" I cried. "Dr Hawkins will be by this afternoon to take the stitches out of your arm. And you shouldn't be out yet. 'Tis too soon. You might slip on the ice and hurt your ribs more."

Da stood on the street, the wind whipping his tangle of reddish-grey hair about his face. He stared at me from under his bushy brows. "Yer sounding mighty bossy, Katie O'Brien."

I flushed, hardly believing I'd spoken so to Da. Knowing I was right, I stared back. "But, Da, Dr Hawkins is coming."

Our eyes locked. I didn't look away.

Da's eyes glinted, then slowly he nodded. "Aye. All right. I'll wait for the doctor, but after then, I'm going down to the wharf. I need to get back to work. It's costing me – losing all this time."

I followed Da into the room. It worried me that he'd be going back to work soon, for I knew the Know-Nothings were still causing trouble for the Irish. I sighed. At least Spike Wood and Patch-eye were gone.

I fetched water and put it on to boil, then started peeling the vegetables. Da paced about. The boards groaned beneath his restless feet. Every so often he picked up a carrot and bit into it.

A knock sounded at the door.

"That'll be Dr Hawkins," I said.

Da nodded and carefully sat down at the table. I could tell from the way he moved that his ribs still hurt.

Dr Hawkins came in, placed his black bag on the table and his coat on a chair. Da stretched his arm out on the table.

Unwinding the bandage, the doctor said, "And how are the ribs doing, Mr O'Brien?"

"Coming along, doctor."

I watched Dr Hawkins snip the waxed hempen thread he'd used to hold Da's gash together. Then he pulled it out, leaving bumpy, red-rimmed holes on either side of a long, ugly scar. He nodded in a satisfied way. "Looks good." He smiled at me, then started to pack his bag. "It was a deep slash you had there. Katie had the good sense to bind it. Your daughter's tended you well, Mr O'Brien. She could be a nurse one day."

I felt the heat rise to my neck and face.

Da muttered, "Aye, that she could."

After Dr Hawkins left, Da let me help him put his jacket on, then he went out determined to get his job back.

I added seasonings to the stew, topped the coals in the stove, then looked around for something to do. The room was as clean as possible what with all my visits and scrubbing but still dreary and dark, lit by the one oil lamp.

I peered through the crack at the boarded window but could see nothing. A cold draft flowed into the room. I stuffed the crack with a rag then sat on Da's bed with his old blanket wrapped round my shoulders. It smelled of his pipe tobacco and of the wharf, a bit fishy and oily. I yawned so wide my jaw cracked. I lay down and closed my eyes. For once, the tenement was quiet, but for the simmer of the stew and the settling of coals. I felt myself drifting off to sleep.

As though from far away, the whisper of a melody played in my head. Then the words: "Crying 'Cockles and mussels, alive alive o!'" The words grew louder, closer: "In Dublin's fair city where the girls are so pretty, 'Twas there I first met with sweet Katie O' . . . " In my dream I opened my eyes and saw Michael, Michael with red fuzz sprouting on his cheeks and chin. I opened my eyes wider and shook my head to clear it. The image of Michael didn't go away.

"Michael!" I cried, springing from the bed. I hugged him to me. He smelled of fresh air and snow. He felt bone-thin and cold but solid. Real! My eyes teared with happiness.

"Aye, Katie O', 'tis yer brother come back from the west," he said, holding me close.

"You got my telegram then, Michael?"

"I did, and started home the next day."

The door creaked open and Da came in. "Michael!"

"Hello, Da." His eyes opened wide. "Jesus, Mary and Joseph! Ye've taken some beating, Da!"

Da nodded. "Later. We'll talk later." He held Michael by the shoulders and gazed into his eyes. "'Tis good to see ye, son." He cleared his throat and shrugged out of his jacket. "'Tis freezing out there and none too warm in here. That hot stew smells right welcome."

Soon the three of us sat at the table. Da and Michael said little while eating. After we finished, Da folded his hands together and said, "We have some hard news for ye, Michael."

Michael looked from Da to me then back to Da, who was staring into his mug of tea. He raised his eyes to Michael's and said, "Our Patrick, God rest his soul, has passed on."

Michael's face reddened. He sprang to his feet. His chair toppled to the floor. "Ach, no! Our Patrick gone?"

171

"Aye," Da murmured. "He died in Cork. And yer mother's sailing. She's on the sea now."

Michael gulped hard and rubbed his eyes. I knew he'd not cry in front of Da. "Mam's sailing? But 'tis winter."

Da nodded. "Sit down, Michael. Patrick's loss is a blow to ye, I know. And we'll none of us rest till your mam's safely here."

Michael sat down. I reached over and put my hand on his forearm. He laid his big hand on mine and squeezed it. Then Da told him everything that had happened on the night of the fire, ending with how I'd gone for Dr Hawkins. "We paid him, too," he said, his chin jutting out. "The O'Briens don't take charity."

"'Twas good Katie was with ye, Da," Michael said, looking at me.

"Aye," Da said, leaning back in his chair. "Katie, can ye pour Michael and me another mug of tea?" I filled their mugs. Da sipped the hot liquid. "Well, I went to the wharf today, talked to the boss man." He made a disgusted sound. "He told me my job's gone. 'Did ye think now that ye could just disappear for weeks and then come back?' says he."

"But there's other work, isn't there, Da?" Michael asked anxiously.

"Aye. There's plenty of work out there. After I left the docks, I went looking for it, and I found somethin'. I start tomorrow. For now, it's just cleaning up, but maybe later I can do some carpentry. The pay's good, more than a dollar a day. Ye'll have no trouble finding work, son. There's such a need now, they'll not be so many 'Irish Need not Apply' signs."

"But, Da, your ribs aren't healed," I protested.

"They're healed enough, Katie. I can't sit here doing nothing another day. And the sooner Michael and I get

172

working, the sooner we'll be able to rent that empty room at Mrs Reilly's."

I nearly dropped the bowls I was carrying. I put them down and clasped my hands. "Oh, Da, wouldn't that be grand? Mam would love it there. And I could help Mrs Reilly with the cleaning – and – the ironing. I'm real good with Mr Pierce's fancy shirts."

Da's sharp blue eyes glimmered under his bushy brows. "Aye, Katie, and come spring, God willing, mayhap ye could go to school part of the time, like young Sullivan."

I stood stock still. My chest squeezed tight and caught my breath.

Da laughed. His laugh sounded like a bark but a laugh it was. "Best ye be getting back to Beacon Street. 'Tis getting late."

After I cleaned up the dishes, Michael walked me back to the Pierce House. The night was clear and cold and stars glittered high up in a black sky. As we walked, we talked of Patrick and how things had been back in Ireland. I told Michael about Elizabeth's and my sickness and Peg's death.

He stopped walking and looked down at me. "Little Pegeen gone, too?" His voice cracked, "Ah, Katie, she was such a sweet little thing."

We continued walking in silence. Every so often Michael rubbed his eyes and sniffed. I handed him a clean handkerchief and he blew his nose.

He put his arm about my shoulders and pulled me close. "Ye've had a hard time of it, Katie. You're not a little girl anymore, are ye?"

"'Tis true," I said. "So much has happened since we left Ireland."

"Aye, 'tis been a time of much sadness."

"There's been good times, too, Michael." I told him of Miss Pratt's leaving, imitating Thomas telling us everything that went on above stairs.

Laughing, he said, "You're a good mimic, ye are, Katie."

"Now you tell me about the west," I pleaded. "We only got the one letter from you."

"'Twasn't all wonderful. The tent cities that follow the railroad are wild, more danger from them than the Indians. But the land is there. And some day I'll go back."

"And your dream will come true, Michael," I said, slipping my arm though his.

"Aye, Katie O', and, come spring, so will yours."

Suddenly so happy I couldn't bear it, I twirled round and round till I was dizzy. I stopped and hugged Michael. "'Twill be wonderful, Michael. School!"

Michael chuckled. "I can't see the fun in sitting pouring over books all day, but I suppose 'twill make you happy. And, sure as shooting, the day will come when I see ye going off to be a teacher or maybe a nurse."

When we reached the Pierces' courtyard, Michael said, "Katie, before ye go in, let me give this back to ye." He reached to undo the clasp of the chain holding the Holy Family medal. "I know our Patrick has gone to God, but he'll always be in our hearts."

"That's the truth, Michael, but . . . Mam . . . she isn't here yet." The uneasiness that wouldn't be gone till I knew my mother was safe washed over me. "You wear it a while longer, Michael," I said, stopping his hand with mine.

He gazed into my eyes and nodded. He lifted my chin and kissed me on the cheek, the down on his cheeks a fairy tickle.

28

The Long Wait

The December wind rattled the window and sent drafts of cold air into the attic room.

Tired from a busy day, I tucked my icy feet up under my night-shift and snuggled beneath the blankets. But I couldn't sleep. My eyes kept popping open with excitement. Today, when I'd walked down to the docks where Michael and Da were working, Michael had told me about his and Da's visit to Mrs Reilly's last night.

"'Tis all set, Katie. What with Da and me working and you helping Mrs Reilly out, we'll be moving to Charlestown on the fifteenth of the month. Mam's ship's already overdue. Sure it will be here by then. Just think what a grand Christmas we'll have there in Charlestown, Katie O'."

Then, eyebrows raised, he'd ruffled my curls and said, "I met Johnny Sullivan over at Mrs Reilly's. He's right pleased ye'll be living there. Seems ye made quite an impression on the lad."

I felt the heat rise to my face, thinking of Johnny. I'd be glad to see him again. Maybe we'd go to school together come spring. School! It was really going to happen. I'd study as hard as I could. And someday I'd be a teacher – or a nurse! The thought danced around in my head. Sometimes it seemed impossible. But then, here in America maybe it was possible. And soon Mam would be here. I ignored the stab of worry that went through me. Surely, with everything going so well, Mam would arrive safely. Warmth stole through me. My eyes closed. I yawned and pulled the covers to the tip of my nose.

The seaman held a woman's body over the rail. A monstrous wave leapt for it. The seaman tossed the body to it, like a morsel of food to a hungry animal. He bent to the deck for another body. I struggled to reach him but my legs wouldn't move. I watched as body after body plunged to the greedy sea. Then I was in the sea drifting down, down. All about me, bodies sank slowly, long hair swirling above them, bubbles rising from their mouths.

I cried out, struggling for breath. My heart pounded so I thought it would burst through my chest. My bedding was a tangled heap. I shivered from the cold air streaming over my sweat-soaked body.

I lay frozen with fear. Eyes wide, I stared into the dark, waiting for my heart to slow. After a few minutes, I recognized the familiar shapes in my room and the tightness in my chest eased. I rose and poured a glass of water to moisten my parched throat. Chilled to the bone, I straightened my bedding, then crawled back to bed and cowered under the blankets, eager for the first light of morning.

Morning finally came. So tired I felt anchored to the floor, I helped Mrs Plumley prepare breakfast for Mr Pierce and Elizabeth. Mrs Plumley poured a cup of coffee for me. "Best ye drink this, Katie. Ye look like ye didn't sleep a wink."

I sipped the black liquid Mr Pierce favoured to tea. Hot and bitter, it scalded my throat and warmed my stomach. I made a face. "'Tis bitter," I said. I looked about the kitchen. "Has Thomas brought the paper down yet?"

"He'll be here soon. I don't know if it's a good thing, you studying the marine news every day. A watched pot never boils, they say."

Soon Thomas came to the kitchen. As we sat down to eat, he handed me the paper. "I know you're wanting to see this, Katie," he said.

I tore through the pages to the marine news. "A ship called the *Seaworthy* 'went missing,'" I read, my voice trembling.

Thomas buttered a slice of toast. "Your mother's on the *Robert Morrow*. She should be in any day now."

Mrs Plumley forked sausage into her mouth. "Stop fretting so, Katie. Eat up."

I didn't look up from the paper. "It says here that sometimes ships disappear without a trace. The ocean swallows them up. They just vanish!" My nightmare flashed through my mind. I shivered with goose-bumps.

Mrs Plumley reached over the table and took the paper from me. "I'm not sure reading's such a good thing," she mumbled. "Eat up, Katie, and think about all the ships the good Lord guides to shore."

"Aye," I mumbled. I chewed a bite of toast and washed it down with sweetened coffee.

The morning seemed to never end. I went through my usual kitchen chores, then tidied the bed-chambers. If all went as planned, I'd soon be moving to Charlestown and helping Mrs Reilly. IF – IF – IF screamed through my head.

In the early afternoon, I pared apples for a pie while Mrs Plumley rolled out the crust. Her voice broke into my thoughts, "Katie, you're destroying that apple."

I looked at the apple in my hand and saw I'd pared

almost to the core. "Ach," I said, "my mind keeps wandering."

Mrs Plumley sighed. "Child, you've not been much good today. Your mind is down at the docks. Come rest time, I know that's where you'll be off to." She wiped her floury hands on her apron and lumbered to the window. She rubbed a fogged-up pane and peered out. "Things will turn out fine for you, Katie, just like they did for little Miss Elizabeth. Look at her out there having a grand time in the snow."

"I'll miss her, and you, too, Mrs Plumley."

"And the child will miss you, but she'll soon have a new mother and she's bursting with excitement about that." Still looking out the window, she added, "You've been a big help to me, Katie. Once you're gone, you stop by every so often and let me know how you're getting on, hear?"

"I will Mrs Plumley."

"Here she comes, all in a hurry. She'll be wanting a cup of hot chocolate."

The shed door creaked open, then the kitchen door and Elizabeth blew in with a gust of cold air. "Katie, your brother's coming down the alley. He's growing whiskers. They're red. Oh, Katie, your mother's ship must be in!" She clapped her mittened hands and spun about the room.

For a moment I couldn't move. Mam, I thought. Mam.

"Go along, Katie!" Mrs Plumley said. "And God go with you."

I grabbed my coat from a hook on the shed wall and ran to meet Michael. Fluffy white snowflakes spotted his hair and his scant whiskers.

"Is Mam here?" I cried.

He held me by the shoulders and gazed into my eyes. "The *Robert Morrow's* coming in. She'll be docking soon."

I wanted more. I wanted Michael to smile and tell me Mam

was certain to be fine. But he didn't say another word. I took his hand and tried to match his long-legged stride back down the alley to the Common.

As we hurried through the park, a man called to another, "The *Robert Morrow's* docking." The man passed the news to another. Soon men were closing up stalls and heading for the docks. A restless excitement filled the air, reminding me of the night of the fire, the night I'd feared I'd lose Da.

Emotions simmered through me like bubbles in boiling water – joy that Da was well, that Michael was back. Excitement about moving to Charlestown. But underneath was the worry about Mam.

When we reached Commercial Street, Michael and I had to dodge workmen clearing debris from the fire. Michael stopped and looked around. "This is where I left Da working. He said he'd be watching for us."

I gazed at the land stretching down to the water. "It looks like a ghost city, doesn't it, Michael, with snow covering what's left of the burned buildings and just pieces of walls sticking up here and there?"

"Aye, Katie. Mam will see a different city than we did in July."

"And a colder one," I said, shivering.

"Michael! Katie!" Da shouted and waved to us. He said something to the man beside him, then, walking slightly hunched, as though to protect his ribs, came to join us. In silence, we rushed along Atlantic Avenue to the pier where the *Robert Morrow* was docked. A hard, fine snow blew off the water and the wharf was wet and slippery. Horse-drawn carts and sleighs carrying loads of rubbish lumbered by.

I drew into my coat and pushed past some people to catch up with Da and Michael. Mam will be with us soon, I told myself.

A ship's whistle blasted the air. Passengers started down the *Robert Morrow's* gangplank. I couldn't move. I searched the descending crowd, looking for that one special face. All around us people shouted and shoved, pushing to greet loved ones. I thought of how Michael and I had waited and waited for Da. Mam wouldn't have to wait. We were all here. But where was she?

It seemed the stream of people flooding the wharf would never end, but still no Mam. *"There! There she is,"* Da called.

But when the woman turned and we saw her full face, it wasn't Mam. I started to tremble. Had Mam not passed the doctor's examination? Sure and it was brief when Michael and I came over, but some people had been sent back. What if Mam had come down with fever? I blocked the thought of my nightmare, willing it to the back of my mind.

My eyes probed the faces of the men, women and children filing down the gangplank and onto the wharf. Did Michael and I look so thin and dirty, so tired and ragged when we arrived? Some shuffled along, heads down, skeletons with rags hanging from their bones. But most of them, no matter how tired, had a look of hope and expectation on their faces. The women pulled their dark shawls close to protect them from the cold, making it harder to see them. Da, Michael and I pushed as close as we could, then stood watching the exodus, waiting silently.

Was that Mam? I think so. *Yes. It was Mam!* She stepped onto the pier, smaller than I remembered, thinner than ever, looking as lost and scared as I'd felt when I'd arrived. "Mam," I tried to shout, but my voice was a whisper. I cleared my throat and waving wildly called again, *"Mam!"*

She saw us and waved back. Joyful relief bounded through me. I struggled through the crowd, wanting to hug her, wanting to tell her not to be frightened, we were here. I started to run.

Michael's big hand clamped down on my shoulder. "Wait a bit, Katie O'," he said, unclasping the chain around his neck. "I'm thinking 'tis time you wore this again." He fastened the Holy Family medal around my neck.

"Yes," I murmured, pressing the cold metal between my thumb and fingers, feeling the imprint of the Holy Family.

The three of us pushed through the crowd to welcome Mam. Da reached her first. He looked down into her upturned face then gently folded her to him.

When he let her go, I rushed into her open arms and held her tight.

The End